WE USED TO DANCE HERE

WE USED TO DANCE HERE

Stories

Dave Tynan

GRANTA

Granta Publications, 12 Addison Avenue, London W11 4QR

First published in Great Britain by Granta Books, 2025

An earlier version of 'How Do You Know Them?' was
published in *The Stinging Fly*, Summer Issue, 2016.

An earlier version of 'Off Your Chest' was
published in *Winter Papers*, Volume 6.

A CIP catalogue record for this book is available from the British Library.

9 8 7 6 5 4 3 2

ISBN 978 1 80351 246 4
eISBN 978 1 80351 247 1

Typeset in Legacy by Patty Rennie

Printed and bound by CPI Group (UK) Ltd, Croydon, CR0 4YY

www.granta.com

The manufacturer's authorised representative in the EU for
product safety is Authorised Rep Compliance Ltd, 71 Lower Baggot
Street, Dublin D02 P593, Ireland. www.arccompliance.com

For my mother, who hates short stories.

Contents

TOURISTS   1

OFF YOUR CHEST   25

HOW DO YOU KNOW THEM?   38

FORGE WORLDS   56

CRISPY BITS   92

THE SLUAGH   116

DOG MEN   132

AND THE BALLROOM   161

BABY'S FIRST PLAGUE   189

ghost trails   224

TOURISTS

Class getting out of the house. He had no plans and tomorrow off, just pissing the pints against the porcelain. Her American features were bright razors through him and Conor saw her as he left the jacks, still wiping his hands on his arse pockets. Her hair was a cinnabar flame and he was twenty-two and doomed. She held his gaze as they moved towards the same door. He was scared he might have left a patch of piss on his pants. Her pupils seemed tricked out with extra shine and he thought he better say something.

Any craic? Conor asked.

Crack, not my style buddy, she said. I may have some Xanax in the apartment?

He was aware his lips were parted. She raised a finger. He looked at it.

That's not an invite.

You're grand, didn't think it was.

Grand, she said, but it sounded wrong, stretched out too much, made it opulent.

Can I bum a cigarette? she asked and he said of course and in these hanging seconds he held the door for her and she stepped through. The smoking area out the back of Toners was the size of a car park and dressed as if it was indoors. It was filling fast – men in suits and office girls – and everyone panting relief. The pub belched noise. He was only here because Kev worked in the fancy Spar across the way. He sparked the light and she bowed her head to the flame, smoke corkscrewing between them.

Shannon, she said.

The river?

That's not what I meant. But yes.

What?

This woman in front of you. Is also Shannon.

He realized she'd put out her hand. They shook on it.

Conor.

He flicked his smoke then and checked her with a look as she exhaled.

Shannon? Serious?

I know right?

She was grinning and he could feel himself doing the same, his Irish teeth exposed. He nodded towards the back of the yard.

You fancy joining us?

Sure.

We're in the corner there.

OK, we're coming over. Hey Blair!

He'd have hated himself if he wasn't delighted it worked. Blair approached now, as radiantly American as Shannon, holding two glasses of Guinness, her gigantic handbag like the yawning pouch of a pelican's beak. Her bright face was framed by a sheeny obsidian compared to Shannon's flaming shock. As they pressed past the crowd, he felt the city might lend him some luck tonight. He'd broken up with Niamh in August, having frozen her out for two weeks and then asking her to meet for coffee when they never went for coffee in the first place. They'd left what they'd had with unspoken

sketchy plans to do better for themselves. He wondered how
that was going for her. He imagined better than it had been
for him. When the three of them got to the table, Kev looked
up from his phone and rocketed to attention. His eyes darted
to Conor's, questioning, like Conor was flanked by a pair of
Caspian tigers. Shannon sat beside Conor. The girls were
both here for one term she called Michaelmas.

> That's a mad name.
>
> What do you call it?
>
> Not that.

Conor had finished three years in Aungier Street. Being the
first from his family to go to college was a source of pride
at the kitchen table, but being the first to be unemployed
after got less airplay. Kev talked a big game about his J-1, the
dollar shots and storied nights, Hermosa surf and trips to
Fatburger, but these were not the same girls. Kev ploughed
on with his saga, nights in sandy dive bars where their
sunburn-pink posse were quizzed on their accents by the
bulb-eyed natives. Where you guys from? they'd asked Kev.
Crumlin, he'd replied.

> And they go, is that far? And I go to her, you wouldn't
> walk it love.

Kev roared at the memory. Kev could be relied on to keep the
chat up and a dance of glances ensued. The polish off them
seemed faintly unreal. Swimmy on the pints, Kev went off on
one about that balcony full of Irish students collapsing in
California, Southsiders turned into Wily Coyote, standing on
fresh air, looking down. Conor looked at them; they weren't
in Abercrombie. They were in clothes he didn't have names
for. Shannon figured it was time for a real pint, and Conor
went to the bar with her. Inside the original part of the pub,
the dark warm wood lent it the air of an apothecary, guarded

by a ferrety barman. She leaned across the counter and lit up at him.

Hi there. Four pints of Guinness, please.

Coming up, the barman said as he snapped the tap.

And could you possibly draw a shamrock in the cream for two of those? Shannon asked.

No, the barman said.

Excuse me?

No. I won't do that. C'mere, I'll give you directions so.

Directions where?

Temple Bar. It's a dearer pint, but they'll stick a bleeding shamrock on it if that's what you're after.

Her nose wrinkled gorgeously and she turned to Conor and his shoulders were wrecked from rising and falling. Her eyes grew again.

Ah, I'm with him, Conor said. Pints don't need decoration.

She spun back to the barman.

What if, OK, what if I put my own shamrock in it?

Well, I can't call the guards on you but I'd hope you wouldn't.

She beamed at Conor. He wasn't sure where to look. He felt the barman at the corners of their conversation but they kept laughing. When he served them, the barman opened up the hell seam of the election. It lowered her. She stared at the shining brass foot rail of the bar.

I can't talk about that, she said.

The barman grumped but wiped the surfaces. Conor kept his mouth shut. She turned to him.

I just hate his voice so much, she said. I hear him in my skull.

We don't have to talk about it, he said.

Thank you. That's why I'm here. Kind of.

Yeah?

I'm an election refugee.

Swam over, did you?

Very funny.

She said she avoided news from home and trusted in books instead. She told him it got all too much and the amount of now had nearly crushed her, lightly resting a hand on his arm. Conor waited until the barman moved away from them until he spoke.

You getting a lot of that? he asked her.

More than I expected, frankly. Us New Yorkers always hated him.

Back at the table, Kev told them about their gun laws for a full pint then stood. Conor knew he was off to meet his girlfriend but Kev didn't give a reason as he put on his jacket. He said his goodbyes and – unseen by the Americans – left Conor with a silly look, straight men at their campest when raising eyebrows about women. Then he felt they were deciding something he wasn't part of. He checked his phone while they conferred then Blair lifted her coat and bag from off the stool.

I'm ghosting to the library. It was nice to meet you Conor.

Yeah, you too.

The two of them stayed for one more. They ran through some classics. He wrote down Irish place names on the beer mats and she twisted her mouth around the foreign constructions and laughed.

Holy shit you guys can hold your drink, she said. Considering your size.

Hang on a minute, he said and he stood up from his stool, close to her.

You're not vertically challenged, but you're not big men. She raised herself up to his height, trying to look haughty.

You're the right height, she said. We should drink a gallon. Wait, what's a gallon?

She looked it up on her phone and licked the cream off her lip.

Thick ass night soup, she said.

They were the last to leave and they thanked the girl collecting ashtrays.

They moved down Baggot Street covered by the canopy of tall trees. It was Baltic and her face peeked out from a giant scarf. The conversation was a puppy they'd been charged with, and they felt they were leading and minding it through town. They didn't talk about her course. She said she got enough of that as it was. He didn't see much point in going on about being a bar back, or a bar bitch as his brother called it. He was having a ball pretending he knew what he was doing. The flash and rush, when your laughs fall together. On the wide corner of the silent square she pulled him close and shushed him. He followed her eyes. Before them a fox scampered, poured itself through the railings and vanished. He walked her home. It took five minutes. He didn't know the way.

There's like, no street furniture, she said.

Sorry?

Don't be. You're all always so sorry. It's like there's not enough stuff, like in old photos.

She talked about vanished cities. She cared more about Carthage than Atlantis. They were the only two on this corner of Fitzwilliam Square. Suddenly she took off up some steps of a grand townhouse, dark and ivy-draped. He followed and they stood before double doors, white on black and lattice-intricate.

I heard a story about this door, she confided.

What's the story with the door?

So. This is the only double door on the whole square. Why is that, you might ask . . .

He shook his head. He'd never seen this door or asked anything about it.

Royalty can't walk through a single door, she said. Not gonna happen. No sir.

Can't? Won't.

OK, mister, won't. So, the King of England was squiring a young lady here, but he wouldn't walk through a single door. They had to put in these double doors.

Not the most inconspicuous way of doing the dirt.

She detonated her smile again and let out a slow low laugh.

Doing the dirt, she repeated.

She stopped and said she'd learned the number of her apartment a month ago to the day.

This your gaff?

It's not all my . . . gaff. Just the top floor.

He shrugged for nonchalance but felt the show of it.

Nice . . . here, I'll let you go. What you doing Wednesday?

You're taking me for a drink.

Deadly.

I'll pick the tavern and I will text you.

Sounds good, he said.

They shared numbers and hugged. She let herself in. The heavy door brushed along on its draught seal, hiding her closing smile, until it finally thunked shut. Alone, he remembered the time. He bolted for the bus. Town felt gusty with promise and he was good for the sprint and he just made it, panting as he swiped his Leap Card. He only copped that he was smiling when he saw a man scowl at him, and quickly wiped it from his face. The man kept staring. His lip was crusted with scab, crystalline from the glue. Conor looked out the window as the 83 took him past the KCR and home. After the man got off, Conor couldn't help himself and touched his own lips. He went home past the same houses and turned the latch slowly. His grandad would be long asleep, his dad up, Liam not yet home. Before they were moved out, their grandad had a veg shop on Meath Street. Conor had taken him back to see it once, until they were both looking at a coffee shop called Legit. His granny was more sentimental than his grandad. She used to go back for the messages on a Saturday and the songs on a Sunday. His grandad gave up after seventy when his bladder took all the good out of it. Liam was working late as a night porter; his brother said he'd seen some wild shit recently and he was hoping to see some more. Growing up with Liam had been a contact sport, a school of headlocks, digs and dead arms, war when he left the house and war when he wanted back in. Their mam would say softly that she thought she was at a place in her life where she could sleep knowing the front door would be closed. Conor had retreated from the fights and so had his mam, all the way back to Cabra in the end, leaving them a house of men. He went through the dark between rooms and found his dad snoring in front of the tv, his cheeks flashed in blue light. Conor bent down and carefully lifted the zapper off his belly and paused the show. In the kitchen he tried to keep the sink clear.

His brother bounced down the stairs in the morning, a carnival barker in fresh Nikes. He got in Conor's space, threw a fake and Conor flinched. Liam was always making him flinch. Conor's elbow smacked a frame of them all and nearly knocked it off the wall. He straightened it as Liam snorted.

What's wrong with you? Liam demanded, cuffing Conor round the head.

Fuck off, Conor said back but his brother was gone, past him and out the door. Then it was quiet. Liam was five years older, failing his mocks while Conor navigated first year, busy getting picked on by teachers off the back of his surname. Conor hated it but Liam was the sound of the house to him, or what was left of it, Liam and their mam tearing strips off each other, her screaming, I'll lock you outside, and him going, fucking do it then. Conor rubbed his head, hoped there wouldn't be a mark. He'd love Liam to have seen him last night. Liam told him years before, handsy is alright, handsy shows interest. Most of them won't turn you down, he said, the hottest ones especially. Hot birds, Liam said, can't be sleeping alone and they shouldn't be either.

His feet sang from picking up clinking sets of drained glasses in the local. The sweet stale stench greeted him before he was through the door, the soured alcohol punchy in his nose and the same lads with dark-veined snouts who couldn't remember that his manager wouldn't let him pour pints yet. He was still on probation. He looked at her number during his shift. Every five minutes smoking out the back was five minutes less of demented towers of empties climbing over his shoulder. Some got stuck and the wrong twist left them shattered in the sink. He finished at half twelve, sank his free pint and got out before he gave it all back to them, fiver by fiver.

A deep sheepy smell rose off the wet coats on the top floor of the bus and he was hoping the must didn't stick to him. He waited for her atop a thin railing at the main gates. Beside him a student explained to his friend that there was no such thing as zero. When she arrived, Conor told her she should see the place in the summer, the Pav with its posh festival buzz, heads laid on young stomachs, cans in the sun, a streaker cheered across the grass. Some days you could have it all. He left out the bit where they were fucked out by security for not having student cards. She ran her hand along the railings as she went. The stuffed streets were thick with amber foliage mulched into the pavement. They walked through the Green and she talked about a photograph he didn't know that had been taken here. They kicked the leaves.

Fall, she said. We're like cavemen.

She dropped her head, frowned and mugged for him.

Leaves fall. Leaves fall down.

She drank less and she drank wine or glasses to his pint. She walked everywhere. She wasn't impressed by the twin Starbucks facing each other on Westmoreland Street, said that wasn't the multiverse she wanted. Meeting back up, watching her rock with laughter, cosying up, comfy with their legs pressed together under tables. He'd nothing to offer on all the tourist spots she was working her way through. He hadn't been to half of them. Her sentences made little trots upwards. He was hoping she wasn't going to make her lectures in the morning. She thought it was cute that Dublin lads spent college living at home. She was reading The Dying Animal. Pendulous is a beautiful word, she said, but her mother told her she'd be glad of her wasp stings later when gravity turned cruel on the other girls. He wasn't about to interrupt. She asked him to walk her home. He hoped they would run into someone he knew as they wound through the gum-spotted streets of the damp city. Four horse-drawn carriages stood at the Green by a line of grumbling taxis. Fat clumps of horse shite on the road and she loved that. She took his hand as they neared her door. She dug in her bag for her keys while she fixed him with a blade of smile.

You want to cross the threshold? she asked him.

The threshold?

D'you want to fuck, Conor? she said.

Yeah.

He followed her up dark stairs. They didn't turn on the lights. They found each other in close breath, with hot mouths, the soft smack of their lips the only sound. Her hair was in his face and she stripped him quickly as they moved for the dark of her bedroom and landed on her bed and when he slipped inside her they gasped loud as each other. She was as demanding as he'd hoped.

Her flattened cheek on his chest before light found the room. In the morning he woke before her and crossed to the window. He looked past the books and the souvenirs and the face-down picture frame, stunned by the view of the frosted streets below. He'd never seen Dublin like it. She pulled him away from the glass, insisted they were going out for coffee and she knew a place. After, he walked round town nicely dazed, the day scented with her.

At home his grandad smoked and shook. He had been given a biscuit tin for an ashtray to save any more ash getting sprinkled and smeared into the chair from his rattling hands. The dead smell rose up out of the tin. Conor sat down across from his dad and his grandad. He lied when he was asked where he was the night before, though there was no need. They had the news on. His grandad lifted his chin at the presenter, blonde in a powder blue trouser suit, an extravagant collar like rare plumage.

Some look she's going after, said his grandad.

They stuck on the end of a documentary about Easter Island-
ers. Liam was heard before he was seen.

Seen this one. Great bunch of lads.

His brother rocked in, dumped his weight onto the couch
and tapped his smoke into the biscuit tin.

So these lads spend a year of their lives carving a moai
out of a boulder and then if it fell over on the way, that was
it, they'd never get the cunt back up.

Language Liam, cautioned their dad.

Moai? That's what they're called. Seen this one anyway.
Wait til you get to them chopping down every fucking tree in
front of them. There must've been a day they went at the last
one, standing around looking at the last fucking stump. Or
the week before, down to the last dozen and kept at it. Saps.
They watched til the end and when he went to bed Conor
dreamed of Easter Island.

They fell into it quickly. Three times a week, walking the
Georgian squares of the old town. It was early October. She
was on Erasmus and she was two years older. She hadn't seen
her father in eight months. She felt welcome in the lecture
halls and the public houses, in the theatres and the galler-
ies. She was delighted with the Dublin she found, a place for
walking and reading, and drinking more than she had ever
done before. New York, she said, wasn't the same. She needed
a break. She felt like she was always wearing a coat of frayed
nerves, that the last year felt like living under her country, not
in it. She missed the smell of hot nuts roasted and sticky, even
more now winter was closing in. She loved the romance and
legacy of Trinity and the hushed sorries that hung in the air
of the bookshops. She said she liked being ten minutes from
everything. He flashed into future hopes, of Manhattan, the

blocked grids of cabs and canyons stretching past vision, sub-
way rumble and rising clouds from steaming grates. Dublin
was real life, she said. You could feel it here, she said. He saw
that she meant it. He'd seen more of it and he wasn't so sure.
Dublin's better at night, he said.
Cos it's a boozy, nocturnal town?
Nah, because you see less of it.
The tram works had half of town opened up, clogged and
chewed and showing its intestines. They stepped out onto
Nassau Street and watched the Americans clamber out of
the coaches, cameras, box-fresh runners and great swathes
of high-waisted denim. The Viking Splash Tour trundled
towards them. Shannon turned her back to the oncoming
circus, winked at Conor, then jumped and roared back at it.
A child sprung skywards, clear air between him and his seat.
His horned helmet fell over the rail and down into the street.
Shannon was already moving, swooping and now the plastic
horns rested high above the bright brilliance of her hair. She
gave the helmet back into the grasp of the reaching child.
There you go, honey.
You're American! the kid shouted in recognition.
Excuse you, I'm Irish as hell. Check this hair.
She struck a pose and the kid marvelled at her brilliant mane.
They walked on.
Maybe I'll stay here, she said.
Oh yeah?
Yeah. Hide behind things. Haunt the Viking boat.
Sounds like a plan.
She invited him to a night out with her class and warned him
too, but he thought he should go. He thought it'd be a couple
of them, but it was all of them. He caught her little mittened
wave and he knew how to move through a crowd. The group

discussed which books best caught Dublin, best trapped it in autumn amber. Conor thought of cults as he watched their professor, a clever hog at the trough of his own lore. Conor kept his mouth closed. She kept a hand on his knee. Then she vanished for a week. Come Friday he lived with knowing his texts were read and no more. He texted Kev and the two of them got eight cans each. When he finally got home to his bed, he didn't move but his brain had gone Gulliver on him. He felt miniature or vast in his head as scale leapt from toes to planets. He felt another wave. When he slept, he slept for ten hours straight. Not the fear after. The fear was a college thing, this was just, blank. Muttered jabs of conversation below. This would be their grandad's last Christmas in the house. His dad said he knew what the nursing homes were, that he'd spent enough time in one for work, replacing the ballcocks in their tiny bathrooms. Conor listened to his dad tell Liam how alien it is to see a house shrunk to a room, everything on top of everything else. Conor turned over. In an hour he'd be up. In two hours he'd be sorting stinking empties out the back of The Kestrel.

Then a text and he met her upstairs in Kehoes. She was already there, in yoga pose, upright and alert in a cream Aran jumper. She let the book drop into her lap and looked at him full of drama.

Hello there.

What's the story?

She held it up in explanation.

It's non-fiction.

He got himself a pint and sat down in the old room. He watched the pint resolve itself. Turned out she'd spent a week in Galway with Blair.

We went to Inis . . . how d'you say it?

She got her phone out. He leaned in as they checked the map.

I just type it now, she said, this is the problem, everything's done for you.

She talked of the deserted beaches and distant mountains, the crab claws swamped in garlic butter and the scarred hands of the local lads who tried it on with them.

We got some . . . po-tin. Not potion, what is it?

Poitín? he asked.

Yeah. What did I say?

She asked him to bring her somewhere else. They walked up past the Shelbourne and its doorman, then the shopping centre looking like a Mississippi riverboat beached up on Grafton Street, glowing rose in the early sunset. He reckoned the Shaw would be rammed. He took her to P.Mac's.

Inside it was hard to hear, and they made their way past stalks of blood red candles. He had to lean over a Belfast sink to order. He got them two Vietnows and he let her pay for them. It was a mission to find a seat but they found the last dark corner and the noise dropped off. She was saying the next one was definitely her last as he stood. Across the room faces fell into context. Liam and Robbie, his brother's oldest mate, granite skulls surging closer and he was snared in recognition. The pair of them had menaced whole years in school. Robbie used to walk lads over to their lockers and demand access. Lads would walk home because of Robbie, their bus fare in his pockets. Conor knew he couldn't dodge them. They got closer, a musty bang of rollover off them. Robbie leaned in to Liam but did nothing to lower his volume.

Unexpected item in shagging area, Robbie said and Liam roared as he took in Shannon, then turned to Conor.

So who's this wetser? Liam said.

Robbie creased himself, making hyena yelps to the ceiling. Shannon stared back at them.

Wetser, she repeated, trying the word out. Is your mother a wetser?

The lads stopped smiling.

Careful, Liam said.

I'd say she is, Robbie said.

Liam scratched his chin.

Need to siphon the python, Liam announced, and so do you, he said to Robbie.

We'll leave youse to it.

They moved off. Conor looked at her.

Who was that?

Just a lad I know.

Am I not worth introducing?

Here, you're an independent woman.

Fuck you. Don't make it weird.

I didn't make it anything.

She didn't invite him back that night. When he woke he could hear Liam snoring. Amazing he was loud even when he was co-matose. Her friends from New York came over so she wouldn't be alone for Thanksgiving. Town was the colour of pigeons. Late kick-off is still early drinking and himself and Kev had cursed the match and the analysis by the time he texted her.

A reply arrived faster than he expected and Conor stared at the screen until the words composed themselves. He was too pissed to see her. He was too pissed not to. He crossed the Green, wide and silent, and joined them at the East Side Tavern. Inside the bar seemed to him a pyramid of Egyptian gold, reflections thrown to infinity. Her friends were all tall clean angles. They'd been to the Storehouse and Carroll's bags were piled high on the table.

You're not as wrecked as I am, he said, slurring slightly.

I assure you young man, she said, that I am giving it the college try.

She brought Conor over to meet them and Andrew was first up. Conor had only a loose grasp of what lacrosse was but he was sure this lad played it, especially after the handshake.

Conor, this is Andrew.

Nice to meet you sir, Andrew said.

What are you having? My shout.

Some good whiskey? Something Gaelic with that peaty flavour.

I'll get them in.

The barman poured out expensive measures of single malt. He wasn't sure how to say the name on the bottle but the barman didn't correct him. He set the drinks down just as Andrew handed Shannon a present.

D'youse give each other presents for Thanksgiving? Conor asked.

Andrew laughed as she unwrapped it, pulling the ribbon towards her.

No, man. Never. Call this . . . a care package, he advised as Shannon yelped.

Holy shit, she said.

She pulled the professional wrapping off. He would know it was Brown Thomas later.

No fucking way.

Of course way.

Shannon cradled an ancient children's book. A fat delighted baby swung towards the reader.

Yes way. First Edition.

Fucking wow, Andrew.

I think you swear more since you got here, Andrew said

and he leaned back and swung a look to Conor for local confirmation. He shrugged. She had both her hands to her face.
She composed herself.

Your presents are always extra, man.

A modest quest.

This, Shannon declared, holding the tattered book up
like a grail, this is the good shit.

He watched them in the dim bronze glow. Laughter flared
from their table as he ordered more whiskeys.

Is that how you say it? Conor asked the barman.

No fella. You made a hames of it. Y'know what though?
The barman whipped a glance up at Conor as he shovelled
ice into a glass.

Fuck 'em, he said.

Conor nodded and opened his wallet, but Andrew approached
and talked him out of it.

Let me. She's very fond of you, dude.

Go on so.

Conor swirled the butterscotch whiskey around his glass.
The smell softened and widened his nostrils.

She needed a break and she needed some friends. So I'm
glad she found you.

They clinked glasses. Outside, Shannon clutched her present
and offered to walk Andrew, drunk and charmed, back to his
hotel. Conor needed his bed himself and he shook hands and
left them to it. He emptied his pockets getting a taxi home.

The next day they met outside Lemon, facing the bunkers
of the Trinity side gate. The place was loud with students.
Shannon was already there, a Ballygowan bubbling furiously
in front of her.

You getting a crêpe?

Her face turned, like he'd suggested she eat his toenails.

Oh hell no, she said.

She looked tired. He was talking more than her and he realized it and trailed off.

I'm going home, Conor.

Right.

It's the right thing for me.

D'you fancy a proper drink? he asked. A send off or something.

No. Thank you.

You in bits?

I just feel crazy fucking nauseous, OK?

Yeah, bit rough myself.

Nauseated, she corrected herself. Everyone gets that wrong.

Cos you're dying?

A new look on her face after he said it.

I'm dying? Excuse me?

Just an expression.

No, not 'cause I'm dying, because—

Say it if you are like, it's grand—

Because . . . I got Plan B this morning.

Conor felt her watching his blank face. Her eyes flickered.

What?

Oh yeah. Brand name. It was the same shit during the Inquisition this morning and I am not here for round two, buddy. The morning-after pill.

This morning? he asked.

Yeah Conor, this morning. What the fuck? Look, she said and looked away. He opened a new pack of smokes and lit one.

Thought he was a family friend.

He is.

D'you ride your family friends?

Don't say ride.

Why not?

We're not push bikes.

A different word would be the same fucking question.

OK. Fine. Grand, she said, in the way she said it.

She looked tired and she pushed the ashtray towards him.

Conor. Please. We . . . can't. We is so much fun, but this little we, that we got. Things like that break at Departures. Things like we.

He watched a plastic sliver of cellophane curl and twist over its bed of ash.

Then what you gonna do? he asked.

Join a convent, probably. Or move to DC.

One or the other yeah?

Yeah. Nun or lobbyist.

She told him she'd had so much fun and she wished that they could let it rest there. She told him his hopes landed hard on her.

It's heavy, dude. And right now I can't have heavy. I'm on vacation.

She tilted her head, looking more calm than sad, and placed her hand on his.

We'll write letters, she said.

Letters?

Yeah. Actual letters. Ink on paper. Vellum.

She rose from the table. They hugged, then stood apart, her fragrance fading.

Hope your quill game is strong, boy.

They left each other. She went into Trinity. He headed for his bus stop through the milling crowds and when he got to it, he kept going. She'd be home by now. He'd an hour's walk ahead of him and he felt like something she found in the gift shop, something mashed into the ground at Funderland. No one ever wanted a warning sign. He'd have to get on with it, without her laugh, dirtier than he expected and he heard it now as he left town. She didn't know the games of slaps, knuckles puce and livid after or smoking soap bar down the lane or your cousin's funeral. She didn't know his first kiss, circled by cheering kids. She didn't know wearing your brother's hand-me-downs. He remembered staying up watching Universal Soldier, when Liam and Robbie discovered he was the only virgin in the room, turning a nothing night long and merciless. He'd have to get on with it, without the shine of mornings with her. He only knew what she didn't know. He walked past the pitches, the charred scraps, black holes in the green, relics of the night fires. He told himself that she didn't know mornings in the Schoolboys' League, bottles of sugar water, muck on the container floor and studs raking you, young sentries on horses and hard ground ready to eat your knees. She didn't know the times he stole from the shop as a kid, the times you got caught for it and the times you got away with it. She didn't know your best mates gave you the worst bruises. He knew she had all her own and he could guess them wrong now. He passed the corner where he took a hiding, all the betrayals from old mates and he didn't know them anymore, lads long lost to Sydney now and he could mark the houses as he went, plague crosses on half the doors. She didn't know teeth destroyed when he was nine, his open mouth smashed into the hard porcelain bath. How he thought his teeth were so strong til then and never after. Pain that vapourized everything, pain that stopped the world around him. It was Liam pushed him and it was a quick slip from there. She knew nothing of his walk back, as it all came for him huge and tidal like cement poured down his throat and he was back in the estates now. He was nearly at the door when he saw a hulking figure stalking towards him.

Fucking lucky I knew the gimp of you.

Liam held up a bottle of vodka he'd liberated from work.

Nearly burst you, he told Conor.

Liam blew smoke and eyeballed his brother.

Y'alright? Liam said.

Not really.

His answer changed Liam's expression. He threw an arm around Conor.

Get inside you sap.

They drank the gaff dry and played FIFA til dawn. Conor told him the lot. His brother didn't take his eyes off the screen when he spoke and they talked football when they went outside to smoke, flicking ash onto the dark leaves. Conor waited to be passed the spliff while Liam went on rambling meanders, telling his little brother stories to make him laugh, delighting in his most embarrassing encounters, stories that started sexy and always plunged into disaster, one behind a dumpster, one where a cat scratched his bare arse and put him right off his stroke.

Here, Liam said. Look what Santy got.

He pulled his phone out and showed Conor a picture: a stack of flat-screens and Liam squatting beside them like he was dropping a mixtape.

These are mine, Liam said.

Fuck off.

Yeah. Work is throwing out fifty of them.

Liam ran through more evidence, shots of him gurning beside screens.

What's wrong with them?

Fuck all. Getting new ones. Fifty-inch Panasonics.

So what happens to these?

Skip. Or, in the case of your bro, into Robbie's van next week, then up there.

Liam looked up, reverent. Above them the warmth of his room, awaiting the screens.

Just pretend you're surprised Christmas Day.

Grand.

You can have two if you want bro.

Yeah?

You can have five.

Liam said that they weren't going out anyway and it doesn't matter if they don't spend their thoughts on you. You can't make anyone do anything and no one gets to the bottom of anyone else. His brother told him not to hang himself on the one thing. It was never one thing. There would have been another thing but there could be another. He said the best he could know is that he never stood a chance.

Got all my crying done early, Liam said.

Every Christmas was sorry excuses and hell in the pubs. He took the extra shifts but the crush wasn't out in the suburbs. He felt himself banished from town anyway. He worked through the nights and waited up for Liam at the end of them. For a few months she wrote letters like a war bride and when he read them, he covered his hand over the last lines to stop himself skipping to the end. They told him things he knew anyway, stale news long gleaned online. They told him things he didn't know too: that she wasn't sure how things were going with Andrew, but she felt like she was going to keep trying. He faced facebook tests, hovering over her image, knowing he could enlarge her. He didn't get to the Book of Kells that year. He never did. In time he saw what his brother had told him but not before he did to others what he wished was never done to him. Years later, when he could, he told his brother he'd been right all along. Until then he tried to keep his head above water but he found enough of it in his lungs before he gulped up clear air and it was all consigned back, until it was all soft hurt, all memories faded and faint, all bullying each other in the embers.

OFF YOUR CHEST

He was sure that was the cancer now, bristling away in his sack. It was coming for him, a pulsing curse inside him. A young man boiling in Army Bargains, convinced of the tumours ahead. From behind the cash register he felt the shopkeeper watching him, so he made a point of fingering the balaclavas. He read the sign in thick permanent marker – Balaclavas cannot be tried on in the shop. The shopkeeper, large and suspicious in a fishing jacket, saw him looking.

The hygiene, the man said. Some of the heads that do be in.

The young man did not respond. He could see the shop-keeper's barbed watching in the square tile of mirror, past the knobby rind of his own forehead. There was no counter in the shop, the owner's shifting bulk on a camping chair down the back like a chief of a nomadic people. He stalled to take in the tactical elite gloves and the digital camo hanging from the ceiling. He paid in cash and shoved it all into his rucksack and was gone. To his left the street narrowed towards the old fruit market. To his right Capel Street blared its ragged day. He lit up and sucked on a smoke. He thought of his mam every time he had one. They had blood and lungs in common. She had only tried to warn him off them the once. It's an itch on the inside, she'd said. An itch you can't get at.

That one time she had gone on holidays, that window before everything, when she still tried new things, she brought back cheap smokes from Crete for the two of them and that was it. On the street, he clamped on his headphones, the dearest thing he owned, and returned to last night's show, right from the top.

– You're listening to Off Your Chest with Clive Geoghan. We're talking to Niall, who's separated from his wife. They've got a young lad and for a play in school their little man was dressed up as a fairy. Would you have a problem with that? We'll hear from Niall next, who's absolutely hopping about it—

He'd been onto Clive for a while now. He had the measure of him. He pictured Clive, his face locked in a sneer behind a studio mic, the kind of man who liked fitted shirts and younger women. Online they called him Jean Claude Van Ham but fuck them too, soft and safe behind their screens. The world was plastic and plastic could be bent to will. He slid his pinky underneath the cellophane of the fag box and worried the corners.

– Niall, you're live on Off Your Chest. You're fuming, are ya? – Steaming, Clive – You're a steamer, Niall? – Don't act the maggot with me – Listen I'm only yanking your chain – No, listen, I'm . . . sorry Clive. I'm fucking furious to be honest with you, Clive. Let me ask you, would you want it? – I've no kids, Niall. Or none I'd own up to, let's put it that way – But if you did . . . – If I did, the rules would be clear under my roof . . . The rules would not be allowing for any fairy dressing, d'you know what I mean?—

He moved through the slate city. He stuffed his hands deep in the pockets of his anorak and went past the Korean restaurants and their karaoke caves, past the nail bars, the headshop, the sex shops, The Brothers Dosirak and the student-packed coffee shops and the bedsits and stockrooms above and then the air owned by gulls. The traffic lights held him back. He ran one nail under another, a thin worm of grime he couldn't get at.

    – No, you can't be carrying a shagging crossbow around in public – I can. I can, Clive, and I will. It's nothing for me to say that I will walk that crossbow into your yard and then we'll see who's a big man, won't we? It's nothing for me to say that nothing at all – Try it! – I'll bring a world of murder to your door . . . – Go on, I'll stick the kettle on . . . – I'll find you. Only small, Dublin. And I do be everywhere . . . – That's enough you, apologies for that, listeners – Everywhere I do be . . . – Can't be . . . – Everywhere . . . Threatening other callers . . . Maybe there's other stations you can do that, but there's no place for that here, that's not us. We've got some standards on Off Your Chest. 1800-466-466. Call us. Few ads to pay the bills now, back after these—

He would never have to see his manager again after this morning. First level complete. No more taking deliveries off grunting Georgians. No more stockroom. Before he saw the light of Christ, his manager had gone hard for a decade in speed and squats. Now reformed and six years clean, he had no mercy for anyone, which made for a prick of a boss, a disembodied voice shouting catalogue numbers into his skull. Getting the sack hadn't taken long once he stopped responding to the orders. It was so simple, something he could imagine his dad doing to his mam years back. Maybe that was where he had got it but he was sure he would remember. He remembered everything. He knew nobody else in a Dublin stockroom knew catalogue numbers like him. Ian, who he had to share an hour with on swap-over, barely knew how to tie his own shoes. It was Ian who first put him onto Clive's show, who said the stockroom was like being in solitary otherwise. He hated the shared hour with Ian, preferred when it was just himself and Clive as he made short work of the boxes. After four years he was dynamite with the knife, the solid weight in his palm and the blade eating everything in front of it. This morning he was samurai slick and he'd finished everything earlier than ever and stood still in the centre of the freezing room. He stopped responding to the orders coming in from the bright shop above. After half an hour his manager stormed down the clanking steps and flung the door open.

Right, what's the story? Why d'you ignore me?

When?

What the fuck's wrong with you?

I just. Don't hear you.

You don't or you can't? Is it medical?

No.

An hour later, with the shop humming during lunch hour, he did it again and he heard his manager finally snap above and he heard him coming as he took the stairs down two at a time, charged in and fucked him against the wall, the tendons of his neck like pale wings stretching to tight ridges. That was an hour ago now. He followed the tram tracks that led past the National Leprechaun Museum and he took the escalator up into Jervis and made for Currys.

– That's not fair now – D'you really believe that? Listen an alien wouldn't believe that – We're all aliens Clive, when you think about it – D'you reckon so yeah? Elaborate on that for me now – To someone else we're all aliens – Come here til I tell you something, can I say one word – If you kept it to that I'd be delighted. – Would ye give me a fucking syllable here? I'm going to say one thing, right? Just let me say one thing – You've another thing coming – Who're you anyways? Here, are you doing a line with the crossbow fella? – Come over here and say that – I don't believe she has any affiliation with Crossbow Joe – Don't be encouraging him. He'll be back on – Ah you're grand. I'm happy in me nappy here— He swerved the minigougers at the Luas stop. They each kept a hand down their kaks while smoking, their weed dank and reeky in the breeze. He didn't want their attention, knew how they saw him, knew what they could do to him. He remembered walking back into his estate the first week of school. The first time they asked, d'you want your go? The second time they didn't ask and there were many times after. His dad had insisted he wasn't going to the local school which was a good way to get the head slapped off you just before you got home. He listened again to the city angry.

– This is it now, Clive. Between Pluto and the dinosaurs, nothing's what it was – Run that by me again now – It's all change, Clive, the dinosaurs we grew up on don't exist anymore they've changed all the names on us they're only cut-and-shunt jobs by these archaeologists – What has this to do with anything, Clive? For the love of all that is sacred and divine, tell me – Taxpayer's money is what I'm concerned about – Dinosaurs don't pay tax, you sap—

Someone had cried live on air once. A grown man giving it the large portion up until Clive called him a bad father. A chesty roar and ugly wracked sobbing.

– Should we ban pyjamas from shopping centres and forecourts? That's the question for the next half hour. What do you think? Let's be honest, it's young ones that do this, isn't it? And sometimes not so young. But it's not men doing it. Now I get the feeling, just a hunch on my part, that decent people are sick of it. But maybe you feel differently. For me, this is about toerags and skangbags—

He went past the deep freezers and ice blue neon of the Asian shop and into Spar and got a can of Monster and had the new box of smokes already ripped open before he was out the door. The stench of petrol and sugar roared up out of the big can, his third of the day. He lowered it down his throat and it fizzed back up from his belly and he let a huge gurgly burp ripple out of him. His mam hadn't rang him today. She'd be off work at six. He checked if she had put anything up on facebook today. Nothing yet. He'd been scaring her more and more recently. Last week, when he had returned after days of not being home, she stood, smaller than ever and further off, looking out the window at the concrete blocks of the garden wall they'd never painted. When she turned, he'd seen her eyes glassy with tears. She hadn't spoken to him since. Now he got what she used to get from him and even with his dad gone, round and round they went, like blood down a sink. She hadn't been onto Clive recently. Last time they laughed at her and told her she couldn't be on every night. That was three weeks ago. He had good battery on his phone.

– Young ones can't be going around doing that and expecting men to behave normally in public – It's a free world or at least it used to be – And you'll be out there tonight parading it round with everything hanging out – You don't know what I'm at tonight – I can see you already – Are you fucking clairvoyant are you? – Common sense clear as day is all I have – Not that common is it but? Open your eyes – My eyes are open they're never shut – Are you a fish, your eyes never closed – A what? – Yeah a fish and a fucking prick too—

He lost a few minutes on Grattan Bridge watching a man empty his suitcase into the river. The contents took to the air. A woman went over to the thrashing man, but he pushed her away with a clumsy shove, then looked to the sky as the papers swung wild on a gust, finally coming to rest on the dark glass of the river. The sluggish Liffey chewed them up. He waited at the quays. When the 145 pitched into view he lined up, stepped on and pulled himself up the stairs, the steps steep in his face. He sat with his rucksack on the seat beside him, as the bus rolled into traffic.

– I know your type – I'm not a type. You don't know the first thing about me – There's thousands like you – Excuse me? – Getting your hole and getting the state to pay for the results – Excuse you? – Here, you're the one up in my business – Wouldn't want to be near your business, wouldn't know what I'd catch – How dare you talk to me like that! – You can probably walk down both sides of O'Connell Street at the same time—

It went on and on as the bus left the old parts of town. There were rumours of a huge black cat wandering through Stepaside and the low hills of the Dublin mountains. Was it right now roving the retail parks? Was it right now sniffing the tyres of a Lexus while an affair heaved in a bungalow beyond? Or hosing out a massive piss in a granny's garden, the steam lifting through the leaves? Clive had a lad on who kept a pair of mountain lions, six vipers and one Gila monster, the exact location of which in Westmeath he would prefer not to disclose. You could rely on Clive for these lads. The man with all the beasts said he should be able to keep whatever he wanted. Bang on, Clive agreed. He ripped out his headphones every ad break. He despised the jingle. The bus powered up the dual carriageway. The smell was at him again.

He was manacled to his own history, in that everyone had the same hot bad intestines, in that there was always shards of wrong snagging inside him. The bus shook and chucked its way along. He watched kids in school uniforms get on and they swarmed the top floor and all around him they talked Irish and he didn't understand a word of it and he put his ears back in.

– They're only spongers, d'you hear me Clive? – A pox A God-honest pox. My God – Thousands coming across the Med – Listen to you, 'the Med' – It'll fill right up – What's that? – Stacked right up. Octopuses and Muslim scroungers and the rest of them – Let it fill up. I don't care. Fill it up – Then they'll only drive over – You be careful with your mouth and what creeps out of it – This is it and when they're bringing afflictions of all kinds into the country – We won't know our country soon – My poor head is wrecked. I do it for you, listeners. I'm a martyr—

The bus left him off at the concrete sprawl of an old shopping centre. He had time to waste. He slunk across the car park towards the diner, floodlit bright inside. He pushed open the door and the blast of hot animal fat made his nostrils flare. He sunk into the red vinyl booth and his table shone with grease. The waitress scratched out his order, hot dog, no sauce, no onions and a large Coke. In the rest of the diner only a father and his son. The father drank a coffee and swiped things on his phone as his son picked at lurid cheese fries. The waitress clanked a second milkshake vat down in front of the boy, the fake cream nozzled on top. He could listen to the show again but he knew he wouldn't. When she came back with his order he bit into his dry dog, the mottled pink showing within the casing and he swallowed and looked around him. The kid had pushed away his smeared bowl. He stopped chewing when he saw what the boy held in his hands, the weight of the book unwieldy. He hadn't seen one in years. The rest went distant now.

He was back in his youth spent scuffing the carpets of Games Workshop, dodging the over-friendly ponytailed and acne-cursed lads who worked there. He spent hours in that small shop. On the bus home, scared to read it out in the open, he would anxiously sneak peeks at the drawings in the Codex Imperialis, shadowed in the dark of his bag. This was when he first saw into another world, felt it expand beyond him, planets and legions swarming in battle. The huge lore of 40k between the pages. Hopeless mortals ruined in broiling seas of war, crushed under the hordes even as the towers fell above, his talisman in the never-ending week and he filled the margins of his slabby schoolbooks. But as he looked at this new cover, he felt no echo of familiarity. He was knocking on air. From the cover alone it all looked false, nothing like what he remembered. It was just shiny fake CG, all gloss and bollix, all cheap nothing, all the shadows flushed out. No room for fresh magic and no new stars to reach. He fell back into the sanctuaried space of the classroom at lunchtime, poring over rulebooks with Hambo, an orcy lunk of a lad with the worst underbite in Dublin 14. When they were mates. Until the door handle was plunged down and the two gentle boys on the floor shrank. Until clumps of mud flew from lads' shoes into the figurines. Until they stamped everything to bits, his armies lying smashed beneath him, the hours of intricate brushwork destroyed. Then it was all swept into the bin and the bell rang and Hambo said he was done playing and he stuck to it, too. All he had now were the ruins of before. He saw it all again but amongst the wreckage, an echo from an earlier age. The huge axe of a Chaos Knight, a HeroQuest classic, the first game he ever had. Now the paint-daubed figure held a crude majesty over him and all he knew, cathedrals of hurt, towering cities bleached and raging, untold billions lost in worlds of ash, every war a grain of sand lost across the cold galaxy. The Axeman rose, the warp storms raging.

Out in the suburbs everything was still and the colour of seaweed. He heard his own breath, saw it turn to live frost then nothing in the black air. Past The Butler's Pantry and by now he was used to the houses around here, each of them grandly named, too good for numbers. A brittle, windless night and the moon fringed by clouds. His mam had been on Clive's show eight times in all. She had been mocked on air and in Tesco Express since, even in her beloved local. Her fingers clicking like insects on the counter, the nails chewed to the quick. He thought of her skin tight from the fags, little bubbles under the eyes, a desperate woman left on hold too long. She would ring in and they would take turns with her.

– I am and you're lucky to hear from me Clive. You called me scum – You must have deserved it – You let me say my words – You're not able, nothing to do with us, love, help yourself – You're not being fair to me – It's only shits and giggles love, yeah? – Would you listen – All right, calm down there, bottle bank . . .–

His mam became a sour joke they kept telling. She was desperate, gagging for him. He remembered her in the kitchen, pleading with him that if she got a few minutes on the air that'd sate her.

I'm allowed a bit of switch-off time, she told him, the ashtray between them.

Doesn't switch you anywhere though, it's only winding you up.

Don't worry about it, she said, and tried a weak laugh.

I am, mam.

Don't be. I just need my words out.

He pissed the bed for years. His dad would come in with closed fists. I should tell your friends what you done, his dad said, hammering his little-boy legs where nobody would see. Later his mam told him he'd learned that from what the guards had done to him. His dad blamed everyone and never came back. He was sure he would run into him but he never had and somehow, came to know he never would.

He was moving across the green when he saw her, her eye a shining emerald in the dark. He stood transfixed. He watched and the panther watched him back. She was the colour of midnight and all grace and power, everything immaculate, muscle under a cloak of perfect fur. She purred and it felt like nature rumbling. Humans had none of this, he understood. She melted back into the leaves. He had stood before her and he had not looked away.

He turned onto Brooklawn. Everything looked darkly Californian. He felt the rule of all he had laid carefully in place. He already had Clive on strings, a puppet to the future. The beginning was so long ago now. The first night, he hid down the alley, his mouth tacky from the sugar and smokes until Clive strode out of the revolving doors and winked good night at the security guard. He had watched him vanish inside the multi-storey. Next time, he waited by the exit of the car park and watched Clive's Saab glide off. As the seasons changed, he kept going back. Every trip he knew more. Every night he was closer. Every night he went back to his mam. He reached the driveway. One lamp was on deep in the back of the house and when he stepped closer a security light flicked on. He looked up and noted where the motion sensor was. He let himself go still, waited until it went off. He crept to the window and peered in at cream carpets and huge sofas. He took everything out of his rucksack. He got the tripod up and worked out his angles and then he lay down onto the tarmac like roadkill. He had cleared the table for her this morning. Clean for once, the papers put away, the ashtrays emptied. He had placed the laptop in the middle of the table, facing the door for her when she came in. He unlocked his phone for the last time. Now he hit Live Video, then Go Live. He would leave this for her. He would let her watch.

He did not know how long he had been down there when he heard the purr of the motor. From the corner blur of his vision, he felt the car slow but he still didn't move as the engine cut the night back to silence. Clive stepped out of the car and the door shut with the softest click. Gravel crunch as Clive came closer.

You alright there, young man?

A step closer and Clive went into a half-crouch, inquisitive, his hands on his knees as he bent down, a sea of stars behind him.

This is private property, you know that yeah?

He readied himself, hands on the ground, as Clive peered down at him. He crouched and sprung up until they were nearly face to face. For a celebrity Clive was tall and he seemed to sniff the air between them.

What d'you want? Cash?

He gave no answer. He inhaled aftershave and panic.

I'm friendly with the Guards, OK? I've had creeps and freaks before. You're not the first.

They were both sweating in the moonlight.

Listen if I give you a fifty, will you clear off?

He watched Clive's eyes dart between his.

Spend it on a few beers, Clive said, when did you last get laid?

A glint of Clive's trademark sneer and he inhaled the moment, the rodent fear before him.

Say your mother has to crack your sheets, Clive said.

Clive copped it then but it changed nothing. At the end of the day a Stanley knife is a Stanley knife and it slid zero fuss into Clive's torso and his eyes narrowed, like he was trying to bring it into sense or focus. The awful truth of the wound grew between them. The puncture sucked the knife as it slid out but with vicious force he hiked the blade up through Clive's stomach. The man's hot rich guts fell out of him, the confidences of his anatomy exposed. Clive's knees swung in to each other and he had to grab him by the shoulders. He held him up with one hand and with the other reached inside his mouth. It was hard to keep a hold of Clive's frenzying tongue but once he freed the tongue web with a nick the muscle thrashed about until he steadied and shushed him face to face and then clasped him and stuck the blade up into Clive's long wild tongue. He yanked and yanked then pulled the whole thing out like a bloody mollusc. The Axeman watched him suffer and gurgle and he turned to the camera. He stretched out his arm and held out the grisly trophy for her. This was his chance and he took it and he did not sleep or listen or speak in the cells he was shuffled through as all things narrowed.

HOW DO YOU KNOW THEM?

Weddings, she was thinking. How other people spend my weekends. They were always two-day affairs now and she still felt their aftermath back in work, under King's Cross, back in the frenzied grey mass for the lunch mope to Pret. The mountains of unreasonable you put up with in London. Nine to six minimum and an hour each side on top. At home no one would expect you to hightail it to a pub in Wexford for a pint, but she made equivalent trips, everyone did, ninety minutes on a Tube on a Friday night, already tired from the afterwork drinks, pressed in as carriage doors slammed and all shuttled through stone. At home no one made you stay up the night before your own birthday baking a cake for the office, like she'd done for her thirtieth, even though she didn't bake, crying into the flour on her second birthday here. Seemed like punishment for ageing. Her own friends had barely made it to drinks that night. Sinead lived over in Fulham and had two quick drinks and scrammed, up early for a presentation. Impossible to run into anyone here. Everything planned and planned miles in advance and if everyone was in London everyone was never always in London either, everyone was always somewhere else. She stayed on past her normal stop. She was scalded by visions of missing her flight, though she had enough time. Getting the Friday off hadn't been hard.

Everyone was always hopping out for doctors' appointments and she got on with the HR girls, who everyone called girls, though they were all in their late forties. The whole office seemed pregnant.

He could never sleep on planes. He made his way through the airport, moving listlessly through perfume and chocolate. He looked at things in shrink-wrap in the fridged shelving of Costa and was upsold a large Americano. These flights were sucking the good out of travel. Three years of only flying between London and home. He queued and he yawned and he was on the same red-eye back as other lads going to it. He didn't recognize them until later but he should have known, there was only four hundred people in Dublin. In hindsight he was surprised they flew from Gatwick not City. He flew out of City once, less a plane, more a posh bus ferrying success back and forth. But then this early in the day they weren't coming from Bank. The Ryanair bag gestapo saw them coming and had each of them try to squash their carry-ons into the regulation space. Undeterred, they pulled on two jumpers each until it was like a posse of Michelin men boarding the flight, roaring, laughing and sweating hard with the layers.

She was shocked awake by the trumpets heralding another flight on time. Give yourself enough time and you can make yourself early for anything. Outside the window, the little old airport with the original tower swallowed by the rest. She heard the two excitable English girls behind her. She'd accidentally travelled with them for hours now and they'd been boozing since Victoria.

No, you do.

No, you. Go on.

Then, roared in an accent that needed only a nylon orange beard, one of them let fly:

Potatoes!

The plane was mortified. She listened to them elbow each other before it was squealed again.

Potatoes!

The two girls collapsed into each other in giggled shrieks. Everyone stood before the doors were open, stooped under. She was back for the one night. Rob and Ruth were getting married. Rob she didn't know, only from pictures. The airport would be the closest she'd get to her parents. Ruth had given her a plus one that would go unused. The only time anyone asked for your address, you knew what that meant. As far as Ruth knew, that was her first London address. Ruth would know nothing of the rat's nest from last year. She hadn't been back since Christmas.

He was back for two nights and an hour after landing he watched the quays through fat raindrops on the Aircoach windows, the Liffey sunk between slimed walls. He got off the coach and walked home from the motorway. He dug out the keys not used in months and he only needed the latch. His sister was where he'd last seen her, on the couch, the beaches and breaking surf of Home and Away on the tv.

Media Studies is it?

Fuck off.

In real life, Alf Stewart would be a massive racist.

Looks it.

He'd love a prison island.

Before he could ask, he heard the key turn and he was so happy.

Where is he? The prodigal son.

The hug he'd missed. But then they didn't hug him when he lived here. His mam seemed smaller. She might be shrinking.

Told you. Prodigal's not a good thing.

Ah g'way. Well I wasn't the one went to college was I?

He was home for an hour. His mother ironed his shirt and stressed about the presents.

They can't have just money, his mam said.

That's what they asked for.

You could have got them a nice present.

This is the present.

Well, I don't like it, his mother said.

Outside a car horn plunged the street into noise and when it didn't stop after five seconds, he knew it was Graeme and that his lift was here. He swung his bag onto his back. His sister threw him an instruction as he went through the hall.

Ask him if he's still a sap, she said.

Graeme was in the drive, his head out the window like a dog on holiday.

Get in loser, lonely cunts club is go.

He opened the back door, threw his bags in the back, then got in himself.

Name might need a bit of work.

Graeme shook his head hard like there was a wasp in it. Graeme was full of chat about Koreans.

All the single ones meet up in April, after Valentine's, he said, and eat these black noodles.

He listened to Graeme as he looked through CDs that had been in the car since before he left. They knew Rob from school, on other ends of a loose gang of mates. He was no help trying to remember the names of Rob's parents. They agreed on the lads who would know.

Better off out, Graeme explained.

You reckon?

Stay home you're at one of these every other weekend. Graeme was on five weddings for the year so far but it was only the June bank holiday. He knew a lad who'd done a full dozen. Then there were the stags to be suffered, some abroad, some out West. He'd missed Rob's stag. Graeme said it was the usual shit, clay pigeon shooting, the only time in his life he held a gun and still drunk when he did. He couldn't afford the good ones. There was one in Barcelona. One in Edinburgh where they never left two blocks, sunk under the gothic shadow of the castle. The taxi driver told them it was called the Pubic Triangle on account of the strip clubs as they bailed out of the cab. Sometimes there were mini-stags in Wicklow on top, for the dads and the less financially viable, hopping on and off a minibus, full of pints and platters. The chat was on who was next to drop the knee.

As a taxi brought her closer, she saw big lumps of cows, stand-alone houses with columns and the nobbly ruins of half a castle. She wondered had she seen countryside this year. East London was all concrete, but the last thing she was interested in come the weekend was more England.

The owner of the B&B up the road wanted to talk, about anything, about her kids, all flown the coop, one in Dubai and one near Luton. She went upstairs to get changed. She stood in front of a forest of pine bunk beds. She couldn't pick top or bottom. The room reminded her how much her rent was. Being single had turned expensive. Cathy had left their flat the month before to move into a bigger place with the boyfriend. She examined herself knowing she'd finish looking at her hair. She'd got her nails done in Chinatown yesterday, shellac, polish and remover flooding her senses and her head kept queasy after. The vicious silver cycle of grey threads: find them, think about them, grow more of them. She was two years into that war. A little longer: that was April, this was June. She knew that Ruth and the bridesmaids had booked a make-up artist from Game of Thrones and she was starting at 6 a.m. The ones who need it least get the most. Seemed unfair, like giving celebrities stylists and free holidays. That saved some cash at least. Can't reuse a dress if it's someone from school. She was friends with Ruth because of their parents. And then she moved away and Ruth didn't and everyone was back for the wedding.

A long drive columned by tall conifers, then a manorly country pile. Graeme parking the Micra made him think of school, lads who drove new cars and parked them beside the teachers' shabbier models. He knew one of the groomsmen – Shaughnessy – worked for his dad's dealership. Graeme had got a scholarship and still took pride in getting less than the national median points in his Leaving. His dad had run off with the au pair and they had more or less adopted Graeme after that, keeping away from his mother and her chardonnay rage.

They checked in. He showered first and turned on the news. He opened the suit bag. The chill stung him down. He'd brought the wrong suit. Magic, just magic. Probably a cold sore next. He put it on, swam in it, felt clowned by it. He tried to work out what stance looked the least ridiculous.

Whoever gets the ride gets the room, Graeme said, emerging from the bathroom in an almighty gush of escaping steam. He watched Graeme's footprints on the carpet.

Grand.

It was a nice idea. The English girls he'd met were hyper confident. Some amazing sights too. He was blindsided by the place half the time.

That your dad's suit? Graeme asked.

In the lobby half a dozen men sporting identical fitted ultramarine suits. He could instantly see who was used to wearing suits and who wasn't and he knew where he fitted into that. He floored the first pint, elbows on the bar. He glugged the next one over the three anthems, the rugby a solid man crutch. On the flatscreen above them South African ogres with straw blond hair were charging Irish players who seemed small. They watched Sexton, completely in control. The crunch of tackles as talk ran to coaches, school set-ups, where the current team would be when they're forty – hulking vegetables in wheelchairs, they decided – doomed to linebackers' fates. Former back rows whose hands shrank the size of the glass. He couldn't imagine a proposal. Couldn't see how you'd do it. Could already see himself looking up youtube tutorials for advice. But everyone was managing to get it done, so surely it was possible. He'd taken to sleeping with his laptop.

She joined the walk up and the heel clack, the bubbles and the small talk. The wedding industrial complex. The pleasantries exchange. She told herself not to be so jittery, which didn't help. It wasn't her getting married. Stand there, make small talk, clap. These were girls who had their shades on if the weather hit ten degrees. In the event of complete cloud cover the shades were perched higher, nested in their hair. A forest of arms, smiles and introductions. Some dresses were the colours of ribbons. Shiny happy ribbons holding hands. She was matt to their gloss. Most of the women had faces

that would not change, bar the odd nose job; faces that pres-
aged exactly what they would look like in later years and she
felt that was mad and it didn't help that no one else saw it.
She knew this was not the kind of face she had. She knew
whatever happened, she would not be waking up to a new
nose. She would make do with her own, even if it was too big.
Looked grand on her dad.

There were swapped notes on Netflix addictions, on the
adorable crosses borne in the face of husbandly laziness.
Strong handshakes and lads catching up, saying you scrub
up well to each other. The men talked about steaks, cupping
the pads of each other's hands to show which parts corre-
spond to what tenderness.

Everyone checked each other out in the church. They
all rose as the organ took the air and they all looked to the
entrance. Ruth looked stunning, if not like herself. Her beefy
father barely keeping it together, his first child to wed. She
should talk to Ruth's parents later. She always liked Ruth's
mother. Her father was a brash boulder of a man, bursting
out of his suit, with a great booming laugh that seemed
everywhere. His boardroom bonhomie seemed to her the
clearest proof this was as much merger as wedding.

I now pronounce you man and wife, the priest said. You
may kiss the bride. A huge cheer went up as Rob reached in
and held her face.

She always thought she'd marry an Irishman. Maybe she
did believe in The One but if she did, she believed he could
be anywhere at this point. If he were here, would she be a
different woman? Sunday trips to bottle banks. A Harold's
Cross life. Her little sister talked about upcoming weddings
for months beforehand, excited and she wasn't even going.
How many weeks spent negotiating invitation fonts and

starters. All the fuss and they were always grand and always the same. Out of nowhere she started thinking that someone out in the world was torturing an animal and she nearly went home right then thinking about it. Somewhere; she checked herself. Somewhere out here, in the country.

He was with Graeme and the startup crowd as someone talked about Barrow Street.

Yeah, I live and love off it, the man said.

The value of your employer is to be measured in how many free smoothies you got.

Everyone was corralled down to eat, a benignly plush and tipsy herd shuffling into the banquet hall. He let three people go first and he was thanked profusely, then another three and he thought he might do this all night. It was details-competitive beside him with two lads comparing cuff-links. It's bad news when there's a glass each of champagne and stout and red wine in front of you. He spied the first drunk, a younger cousin, no bets taken there. Single lads were giving themselves away with too much eye contact on the bridesmaids, too much time spent staring over shoulders and not enough on the person in front of them.

The table looked up at her. This was not the girls' table. She looked at her name surrounded by names she didn't know. She cleared her throat.

I'm not sure I should be at this table, she said.

Ruth came over. It was only a few minutes. Ruth introduced her to everyone. She sat down and started shaking hands. Found herself beside Helena, three years older, perfect Donnybrook teeth and a passion for The Secret. It had Changed Her Life. It was all visualising. You only had to see it.

On her right was an uncle who looked like a dachshund and a heart attack stuck together. She watched Ruth glide to the top table. She took her seat. Teenagers in waistcoats forked out three types of potatoes onto plates with metal tongs. She saw another goat's cheese tartlet and waited to ask about the vegetarian option.

We have a lovely mushroom risotto, the girl said.
They always had a lovely mushroom risotto and she said that would be brilliant, thanks a million. She could picture the brown gloop ahead of her. People went outside for smokes between courses. She shifted and lifted her head slightly as the speeches started, hoping she looked kind and interested. Only men spoke. The best man's speech was definitely based on a template. Any more directly lifted off the internet and the lad should read out the URL and the pop-up ads. Pools were going on how long each speech would be, schools of fivers fished out and thrust to the centre of the table. Ruth's father stood and cleared his throat.

Terrible birth. Today you see such an elegant, impressive young woman. But Ruth was a real turkey when she came out. Her poor mother. So traumatic. And I said to the doctor, put a few extra stitches in while you're there.
She blinked. Some big laughs, some shocked gasps. She watched Ruth as she closed her eyes and inhaled.

And she looks just amazing today, said her father.
Her father wrapped it up shortly after that, tugged down by his mortified wife. She let her eyes drift around the room.

Doesn't she look wonderful today. If she wasn't marrying my son . . .
The room loved it. She'd no one to nudge under the table.

And the rest, as they say, is history.

She examined the cutlery and thought that yes, she was behind in adult life but the colours of that fact only seemed fierce at times like this. She thought she'd have to make a call on it this year. She wasn't living in London. She was surviving in it. You are what pays you – and not what you did in college. She knew where that fell. She sipped her wine and nearly enjoyed how easy it was for everyone when people left. At home they talked like every Irish son or daughter in London was waging a great campaign of personal achievement, but better weather didn't solve all of it. Keep it from your parents whatever you do. We just got stuck out of sight, she thought. We just got rotted elsewhere.

People had travelled from far and wide and the furthest-flung places were named and clapped. He watched Rob stand for his speech, groomed and immaculate, but nervous too, and in his opening jokes Rob did not seem to enjoy all the laughs that came out of his mouth. He thought of what had been brushed under. How Rob put his mouth on mouths he shouldn't have and how that had been put somewhere else, somewhere no one mentioned. When Rob had told him. How much he hated Rob for that, for putting it on him, snaring him in his Audi with the knowledge. He clapped. The best man stood. The room nodded sagely back as he spoke, everyone's face a cherubic droop, ready to hear the finest about the men arrayed before them. The fourth of the men stood down and the fifth stepped up. He found himself at the bar again. Sharpeners were in play: long eels of cucumber slid submerged between gin and ice. He watched himself in the reflection. Along the bar, girls held court over Rob's hulking younger brothers.

o

Kids flew around at a lower level, another world careening round tables at three foot off the ground. A large circle was forming for the first dance. As people crowded towards Ruth and Rob, she let them pass. She knew enough about how this worked. She excused herself and followed a crunching gravel path through the grounds. Nothing around for miles and miles. There was still light in the day. She could hear the wedding, distant, like an island.

Now it was jackets off and everyone was well on their way. The best man collected envelopes. A chattered sharing about the best spots for 'people-watching' and she felt cold and she felt nasty. She turned and leaned in to the girls beside her.

You know what I reckon? I reckon people-watching is just brunch speak for perving.
One unsteady laugh. Two dropped faces.

So what, like, you hate brunch?

I don't hate it. I just don't believe in it. Like if you're gonna spend a tenner on eggs on Saturday morning, maybe you did Friday night wrong.
That didn't go down too well. She realized she was a bit drunk the second after she said it. Someone put the chat back on track. She got a text from her sister asking how Ruth looked. She wrote back under the table as someone called the music funky and she thought that the only people who said funky were people who'd never listened to funk in their lives. She was too cynical for this. She tuned in to the talk at the bar near her.

It's all binary when you get down to it isn't it?
Of course that's it. That's it entirely.
Beef or salmon. Boy or child.

She turned to her left where the chat was houses, the girls who never thought they'd cross the river but were now snapping up properties in Stoneybatter. Mummy and baby yoga and the party was only starting. She wasn't staying the second day. On her way to the bathroom a girl stopped her.

Your hair is Oh My God.

Thanks.

It's, I don't know, like a hot gypsy look. I love it.

She felt the wine was going to answer this one for her.

Well I'm half Roma, she said.

Sorry?

That's my people you speak of.

The girl looked confused.

No way. Not really?

No. Not really.

Oh.

She savoured the discomfort worming its way through the girl's souring expression.

Why would you say that?

Sorry . . . doesn't matter.

The bothered girl excused herself and left her standing there. Out the window, peaches and corals moved past chased by laughter. She thought that these days – planned for so long then not remembered – were driving everyone mental. She'd heard of a girl going around pricing the rooms and venues even though she had no fella. It was never too early. Looking for yourself and when to give up on that. How could any night solve anything.

He found himself at the bar again. He'd three people in his field of vision he needed to dodge. He saw Rob's dad and looked away. The man's company was like being trapped in a lift. Keep moving. How much had been spent on hair all told in the whole place? A Turkish barber had done his for eight quid, dry cut. The shock the first time the old man burned his ear hair off him. He felt a firm hand on his shoulder.

There's the man.

When he turned it was Rob, arms out. Rob hugged him and he hugged Rob back. Over a pint Rob caught him up on his plans. He leaned in conspiratorially. He said he knew it was horse shit to be getting lessons on marriage from virgin priests but when the time came, they were still getting the kid baptised. The time would probably be next year. Schools decided it, absolutely.

I'm an atheist but a realist too, Rob said.

He was swept into another round, Baroque seas of Heineken. Fresh notes used every time, a climbing hill of coins in his pocket. A clink and a refusal of money, the see-saw of cash grasped. He was in the walled garden as night fell. He watched a glad fat uncle, Falstaff pride whenever he had the groom close and bringing up the stag whenever he could. The talks went further back amongst the lads, back and back into school and summers between, the broken glass in the cocktail-wet sand of a Stillorgan car park. A beach in a car park. He raised his glass until it filled his vision.

She'd been single eight months. She'd been hurt and tender in ways she didn't know was possible since. Some memories were grand. Some eased off and some pierced her at weird and inconvenient times. She thought of her brother Jonny. How he'd rung her - fuck a skype - the night she found herself dumped. Jonny had plenty to share and commiserate over. That was the thing with being gay, he told her. You don't get a chance to fuck it up til so much later. It meant having a teenage relationship at twenty-fucking-four. Wrong people. Not bad people just the wrong people. He was still behind on his mistakes, he'd told her. He said she was bang on schedule and she'd snuffled and laughed through tears and pictured him making that face of his, the revulsion fresh and toxic. He said to her on his twenty-first that he'd go off to Canada and go off the rails and that's exactly what he did. Came back wiser, but quieter too. She didn't know much about what that life was for him. She'd been one of those girls, relationship to relationship, just not right now. She was headed back to the table but then she stood still and let everything move and bounce around her. She turned and wandered instead.

The band kicked up another cover as she reached the bar. He was already there, yet to order another mammoth round. He felt her close by and it charged and raced the space around him. He kept his eyes down, the dance floor behind them. He ran a thumb over the hills of his knuckles. She got her card ready. Say yes to a wedding and hear your wallet shriek. She wondered when using your debit card wouldn't be a gauntlet of nerves.

He saw her in the etched gold lettering of the mirror, through the blinkers of booze but he didn't look straight at her. Across the counter the spotty bar girl landed exactly between them.

Who's next?

They turned. Their eyes met. Time stretched like a cat. His face did a shy brightening hop.

Sorry, he said.

Her skin seemed porcelain pale, stark behind her hair, scarab beetle and perfect black. She looked like someone from a time before fake tan.

Am I skipping you? he asked.

Her face held him there, suspended.

No, you're grand, she said.

He was coarsely handsome, mumbly lips. Don't slag his jacket, she thought. State of it though. Don't be a bitch, she told herself, the room is stuffed with bitches as it is.

Ah, no, I did, he said. You go ahead.

She hesitated. He wanted to say something, something like how pupils were the closest things to galaxies we have, but thoughts tangled and everything sounded like shit dumb muck. Unable to say everything, he said nothing. Her lips parted slightly.

You sure?

Yeah, he said.

Cheers.

They each turned back to the mirror. She placed her hands on the edge of the bar, each aware of the other in profile. The song ended and they didn't speak again.

The night galloped on. Lads playing at ghosts in the hall, the tablecloths over their heads, flying around the room, eyes sunk and wild. Later lads singing up on shoulders and verses lost and mangled but no matter. Past midnight, Graeme and the lads came storming back from the jacks with their eyelids sprung open, forcing through their arguments like bullying county councillors. It all felt like communion and how much did you make and what's your new name. Only a second ago he was looking at himself in the mirror, but now he was suddenly between three doors and outfoxed. He picked a door and he crashed through, shocked by the cold outside. The fire pits glowed beyond, covens of smoke, gags and warmth. It was growing late and it was growing light.

o

She was sore in the morning. She saw a world of pine before she knew where she was. Someone else was snoring. She peered over and saw a lad mashed into the lower bed. A trail of peach-shaded sick snailed around the corpse, slowly lifting and deflating with each snore. A wet pillow flecked with little red chunks. She tried to work out how she would get down.

A walk up country roads and everything strange and bright and quiet. Her stomach turned when she saw lads tucking into full frys, red faces shovelling cooked organs, the middle grey mass of a cut sausage. Back in the lobby of the main house a member of staff scrambled towards a leaving party.

Excuse me? Excuse me?

They turned as the woman reached them.

No one paid, she said.

Everyone swiftly apologised and it got quickly covered. A girl she'd talked to the night before was emptying a pack of Solpadeine into rows of fizzing glasses for couples staying the next night.

I prefer my hangovers with the filters on, the bridesmaid said.

Only one thing for it.

Do the job.

There was talk of getting on the road, of service stations and breakfast rolls. Her brain was banging off her skull wall.

He woke to Graeme moaning softly in the brace position, a can of Lucozade, shiny with cold, pressed to his forehead.

Fucking hell, Graeme said.

The wreckage in his head appeared briefly too much for Graeme and small wounds left his mouth.

This is one for the fucking ages, Graeme said.

Nerves sprang and scurried around her as she queued to get onto the plane. She landed in Terminal One in the dusk of Saturday. Seasoned at this, she picked up a sandwich in Marks and Spencer and watched the clocks tick above her on the platform.

He did nothing with the second night home. He went for the cure with Graeme and when he got in he'd forgotten which steps creaked on the way up to his room. Hangovers like this reminded him of school, when the weekend cowered before Monday. He got a flight the next afternoon. He'd be an adult when he didn't go to Burger King no matter what time it was. No sleep on the plane, spat out by the Tube two hours later and only the kebab shop beckoning in buzzing neon. He ate beside taxi drivers and families swaddled in white robes. He checked his phone. The lads would still be up. He'd make Match of the Day 2. He walked up wet dead streets and into his flat.

They lived within a mile of each other for two more years. They never saw each other again though they shared some shops. They don't know this but we all have it carved.

FORGE WORLDS

Oran had survived worse and he couldn't hide it anyway. He knew the tides and choppy seas of the hangover to come and he wouldn't have his head back for hours. Ger, across from him in the van cabin and ten years older, had a nose and must have copped the sweet stale punch of ethanol trying to escape Oran's flushed face.

Oran was in bits. He already hated the day and hated the county he was stuck in, the county he had bought a gaff in, and he buckled up. Sure renting is only dead money, he could hear his da in his ear. Howiya bud, everyone in town was always saying, like it was the funniest shit in the world, and everyone in the town called it Howiya Estate, because half of them were Dubs forced down here.

They'd had different nights. Ger and Dearbh finished a true crime thing over a bottle of red and he was up early anyway, tea for Dearbh, kids woken, everyone out the door by half seven. Ger's mood breezily denied the morning grey and he was going to chase this day down, a sharp and frigid Friday morning as he swung the van out of Oran's estate. Ger thought that the songs on the radio were always about tonight.

Not enough songs about great mornings, he said.
After the news Ger reached for Spotify and Oran could guess the songs.

Grumpy bastard Van Morrison, Ger said.

Oran blinked in venom.

Imagine how bad he'd be if he actually was cleaning windows for a living.

The joke was lost on Oran but Ger hummed away. He liked what he liked and Dearbh indulged his hobbies, soft pursuits she called them, gathering up useless information. She did not understand why you'd need to read a book about the making of an album, not just listen to it.

Ger saw no point in telling Oran anything. The lad seemed reluctant to grow out of his daftness and leave the noise of the nightclubs behind him but that was his business. Ger's niece Eloise was that age, and she was something mad to him, full war paint to so much as go to the shops. They were impossibly confident, back home on the weekends thinking they invented college. He guessed his own two would face these rites soon enough and he was happy it wasn't this week. For Oran the day was already survival tactics. Felt like he'd had his head on the pillow for a minute or less and now his mired brain was a flaccid slug.

The van stopped outside The Seum, the scene of the crime. Oran watched the cleaner in a fleece smoking, wind-whipped and rickety with the cold. Her neck had the sharp movements of a hen, cocking her head up to finish her fag. Oran looked at the purple doors, where he'd poured his time and their money hours ago. Stepped down in the basement of a midlands hotel, The Colosseum Nite Club was Roman themed, imperious faux marble busts guarding the entrance by the coat room, opening up to a cavernous room facing a massive diorama, the gladiator bang in the arena, looking up to the vestal virgins with their thumbs all pointed down. Eloise wasn't there last night. He wondered if she would show her face tonight.

How's Michelle? Ger asked.

She wasn't out.

She's more sense.

It'd been years since Michelle had gone out on a school night. She called the club The Vomitorium and when she did venture out it was well outside the walls of the town. Oran had been slower to turn his back on the place. You couldn't wait til Friday, he cursed himself, that was all it was, him and half the plains around.

Ah you couldn't be working as an SNA with a head on you, Oran said.

Still biting, are they?

Bite you when they're happy, bite you when they're sad, or they haven't slept.

We don't pay them enough, Ger said.

Getting battered in work. Be fucking funny if it wasn't your missus.

She'd learned to only hug them from the back. She told Oran girls got diagnosed with autism way later. Girls were better at assimilating, fitting in and hiding things. The parents were always in a state, begging the school to take them and the Department was a nightmare. Michelle said it was only the other women there made it bearable. The Wailing Wall, one of the older ones called it, the low wall where the SNAs went for their smokes and breakdowns. She was leaving earlier and earlier every morning to get back to town and she called it clutching not driving. Oran had found out that early goodbyes meant goodbye to rides in the morning. She was gone by the time he was up. Beside Oran, Ger made an interested sound.

Used to be a Supermac's there, Ger said.

Yeah?

Ger was remembering the night years back, the windows smithereened across the pavement in jewelled bits.

Youse are all mad for it, Oran said, who had nothing against Supermac's, only it was for boggers and train stations and boggers in train stations.

Tell you who's missing them, Flynn Glass. Probably paid for his villa in the Algarve just on the replacement sheets. And he in a new Merc.

Oran bit his lip and Ger moved on to chatting amiably about the most maddening aspects of teenagers. They seemed to only wear clothes that didn't fit, on purpose. The lights glowed green and Ger moved up the gears. All around, Carlow and Portlaoise, towns planned to keep car parks happy. The meat plants with the Romanians packed into the bungalows. Not enough going on but everyone in each other's business. Affairs happened in thin air, spread from one mouth to another, half seen or invented on Saturday and fused into fact by midweek. A place made mean by the cold and gossip was the beast that ran the town.

Oran looked at his phone and clucked nastily. His battery was low, a sliver of red and no more. He'd forgotten to charge it when he went to bed.

Need some juice?

Yeah.

Ger passed him a phone charger.

The smart bear plugs it in the night before. But you know that.

Thanks Dad.

Ger grinned as Oran plugged the cable and adaptor into the cigarette lighter.

Have you anything booked for the summer? Ger asked.

No. Not today's problem, Oran said.

He had been holding off booking them a holiday. The lads told him that a holiday at this stage, after living together three years and not a dog to show for it, would be taken as The Proposal Holiday. Oran didn't see it as clearly defined as that but he wasn't going to be taking the chance. This left him pissed off at the weather and to a marginally lesser extent Michelle, and they'd been playing sour tennis with each other since. Maybe forks were getting stabbed into Chicken Kievs of late or maybe he was imagining it, but he saw no good way of finding out. He was a champion procrastinator, always had been. He had never got past thinking that settling down meant settling. They went on like that, Michelle feeling the looks slice her from the girls in the chemist. One night she said she had seen folic acid in Ciara Dempsey's cabinet. Oran said she was the one who was digging in Ciara's cabinet. Michelle had gone to bed soon after.

On their first job together, Ger told Oran how the whole country was covered in trees once, all of it one great sea of oak. It took a hundred years or more to grow trees like that, he'd said. He was always moaning about Coillte. Short-term thinking, Ger said. Most IKEA stuff is only chicken nugget wood, but Oran didn't need telling, he was surrounded by it at home. Oran had never liked being out of Dublin. They'd been serious about woodworking in Letterfrack, but the place was barren of pussy and craic and the first couple years home, before Canada, he was in his element. If it's coddle you're after here you'll be waiting, Ger told him one day. They made a deal after that. Ger wouldn't mention coddle and in return Oran made no mention of the All-Ireland and the Drive For Five. Oran had smirked all through the summer but he kept his word and his mouth shut, as the sports news came over the radio. Ger let the younger man smile out the window, but he knew the truth: nobody should boil a sausage. They both loved talk about the hallowed boozers up in Dublin and that only made Oran more homesick. Ger took the eighth off before Christmas every year and himself and Dearbh would head up and after the shopping was done, they'd retire for a few in the Long Hall and she'd have hot ports while he worried the wood like a pervert. Oran closed his eyes but the crushing kept coming.

The tricolour and the stars and stripes flapped in the malign wind and Ger rolled the van into the car park. In the joinery the day was already motoring, the shutter roll up and Vitali on the forklift, laughing at Oran and shouting god bless the workers. They went past a skip buried underneath offcuts. Extractors piled up hills of dust that made Ger think of sand dunes. He loved the noisy wall of it filling his ears, the roar on entry, the plane desks going ninety. They moved past the orange racks stretching up the double-height space, the CNC machine above in the mezzanine. This was April and the place hummed rabid busy. They'd twenty jobs on. Tommy would be in an hour already, Tommy the machine man, Tommy a dying breed. You think you know it, he always said of the router, but it never knows you, and there's no small accidents. Ger pushed the door to the office open. Inside, Brian Junior, phone sandwiched between shoulder and ear, swept them in with one hand and with the other closed the door over on them. Brian, son of Brian Senior. Ger liked the old man but he never saw much point in Brian. Something in the son's manner put Ger off him. Far as Oran was concerned, Brian was a silly gimp who looked like he'd stuck on a pair of

chinos early and never took them off. Brian made them wait.
Brian laughed loud. They checked their phones while Brian
finished up. He looked brightly at them.

Now. Sorry about that lads, Brian said. That was that gob-
daw Lambert, we're too expensive he says. I am, am I? I says. I
told him we didn't start at it last week. Course we're expensive.
Christ, the Polish are expensive. Get the Moldovans if you want
value. D'you know how long we've been here? I said to him.
Ger knew how long – he'd been here for most of it – but he
said nothing.

Twenty-two years, lads.
And it was a family business. That was the other thing.

And this is a family business, Brian said. We're very proud
of that.
That it was a family business just about crept into truth. Brian
managed the spreadsheets and did all the graphic design and
patronizing for the company. He inspected Oran's broiling
face. Oran met his gaze and took up his full height in front
of him.

You look like you didn't do your homework, Brian said.
I'm not dying, Oran said.
Spectacular news. We're too busy for that. Suck up your
shit lad.
Brian handed them their summons.

There's the order boys.
Ger took the paperwork off him. They hastened their jackets
round themselves as they stepped back into the bite of day.
Wet church car park on the back arse of town where school-
girls shared smokes and bags of jelly snakes. Ger recognized
one of them, older sister of a girl in Jase's year. A lad in
the leaf-damp square made three hundred quid in front of
everyone out the back of a black Honda. Ger steered the van

around Shaws on the corner. He liked the precise size of the old slogan, Shaws – almost Nationwide, but that was gone now. The van moved out past the plant where some of the lads Oran half knew from the pub worked. Ger was detailing a local scandal, telling him about the fires that took hold in the back field of a developer's farmstead. All the years of paperwork gone up in smoke and left in flaked and smoking carbon. Cowboys don't keep records.

Out past King Oil and as Ger wound the window down the punchy whack of slurry swept into the cabin. Smell always made him think of Ollie McCormack from school, who'd got up early and died on his own family land. A cloud of evil gas lying in wait underneath the barn, everything the animals rid themselves of over the winter, and young Ollie swallowing fumes and pig shit, asphyxiated. Ger had sat beside him in school for three years up to the inter cert. Silos ahead and bunched and bagged bales behind Ger as he nodded at the horizon.

There's the weather, coming up country.

Rain was around, the soft always menace of it, rain that splashed or stung, rain that wished it was snow, rain that barely bothered, bored of itself and everyone under it. They rumbled past Dowling's with its enormous car park that would be full that evening. Ger insisted on the news at eight and Oran closed his eyes. Michelle would be on the M50 by now, halfway back to Dublin. They'd spent five years out in Toronto. He'd get on a plane in the morning. They'd only come back for Michelle's dad and his shocking incontinence. Canada had been good to them. There was space out there, vast skies and unreal money. That was living. Mental different species of tree over there, even a purple wood once, purpleheart they called it.

Roadside cottages and low walls passed. The national pallor was steady here. They were within fifty miles of Barack Obama Plaza. Furrowed dark ditches ran behind them. Country music as they appeared briefly on the Old Carlow Road. The van whooshed the bend and gravel spat onto the crinkled plastic and pink flowers greying on the side of the road, Carmella Byrne in the ground nine raw weeks before her twenty-first birthday. We will not return to her.

Ger brought them into the nearly finished estate, a hundred and ninety-seven units going up, all two and three beds. It wasn't the worst install, or the most interesting, hanging doors and fitting windows, the first fix was done and the sparks following on. Gaffs Oran couldn't afford himself and he tried to think past his curdled head. He had seen a lad kneecap himself over in Canada, swinging down off a beam like an orangutan with a nail gun and putting a three-inch nail right through the hinge before he touched the ground. He plugged his phone into the wall, feeling Ger's eyes on him. The two of them went hard at the work, their hands dancing with expertise. Oran watched the tip of Ger's tongue poking out like a little fish while he worked, Oran sweating it out. They downed tools, and Ger kept one hand on a finished turn, appreciating the care gone in. For a second Oran could glimpse past his bad head and there he saw Ger cleanly, his view of the work and the quiet pride of the man.

There's some lovely work, Ger said.

All yours, boss, Oran said.

Compliments made Ger itch but they both knew it was true. He blew into his mug of hot tea.

Supán tae, Ger said, smacking his lips.

Oran needed to climb out of this and he cracked and started

downing a full-fat Coke, and felt it fizzing up in him. Aggro sugar bubbles raced down his gullet and he lit a smoke as Ger scrunchily bunched his sandwich wrapper.

It was ten past eleven when Ger moved to the router. Oran crossed the room. Ger flipped and handled a cut and fed it in just as the toe of Oran's runner snagged under the trailing cable of the phone charger. His foot was yanked back behind him and he lurched and not meaning to, reached out to steady himself and Ger was the closest thing in front of him. His hand planted on Ger's back and pitched Ger off balance and then ten things at once and the saw bit and he was pulled straight in and a noisy high whine off the router blade then sawdust kept coming, kept spitting back into his face, blinding shard attack and the whining blade drove into the grain, and a bucked-alive kickback hit, smack of recoil and torque and the saw flung itself up out of the wood and its teeth flew clean through the top of Ger's finger, slicing-gone, skin-nothing. The entire silvery sinew flew out of his finger like a bit of silly string and whistled around the room. The top of his finger fell into the sawdust and the sinew drifted down after. The air turned to a fine mist of blood spray and fell flecked and hot on his face. His legs went. His knees took the fall and he slowly keeled over as Oran ran to him.

The lines on the floor of Portlaoise Hospital told Dearbh where to go and she followed them. Jason was trailing behind with a balloon, never before outpaced by his own mother. When Dearbh saw her husband in the room alone, propped up between the railings of the bed, he looked out of place, like a seal in a zoo. They didn't speak. Ger sat up, slow and huffingly awkward as he raised himself on one elbow, unsure of his hand, hidden in fat bandage. The tip of his right index

finger. He'd never had an accident before and it didn't matter now. Dearbh got herself a chair and positioned it by his
bedside, and sat. Jason stood in the doorframe with a balloon
bobbing against the ceiling above him.

Give us a minute Jase, Ger said.

His son took himself out of the room, yanking the balloon
down as he retreated under the door. Ger looked at his covered hand.

Just climb-cut my own finger off.

Stop beating yourself up.

Two fucking stupid decisions—

Jesus Christ. Stop.

She brought her face close to his and they looked at each
other again.

Heard this rotten scream first, he said.

She bowed her head to let him speak. He had no more to
say.

Shouldn't have been you Ger.

And I was sat there thinking who in the name of God is
making that racket and then I copped. It was me.

He could only think how perfect things were, this morning.

If I could change it, love, I would, she said.

I need one for the other, Ger said.

She rubbed his good wrist, staring at his hairs. His gorilla
arms she always called them, the same black hair that came
over his back like woods on a mountain.

It's not typing, he said.

I didn't say it was.

Says it's months before I can do the basics with it.

That's not bad, love. I expected longer.

Yeah well, your iPad isn't a doctorate so I'll go with what
your man says.

She sucked her lips in and he looked out the window at the pebbledash of the hospital walls. He was never sharp with her.

Sorry, he said.

We'll manage.

He reared up with it.

I need more than the basics Dearbh—

I know.

I'm all in the hands.

There'll be a knack to it and we'll find it. Right? We just need some grace under pressure.

She looked at him dead straight then and he paused.

I'll give you a hand, she said.

He blinked then as she buckled with her own laughter, brayed, gulped for air and kept laughing.

Jesus Christ—

Ahaa . . . sorry.

Dearbh.

I'm sorry.

But she wasn't and her mouth spread in bold delight. The nurse came in and watched, Dearbh covering her mouth and still giggling. A hint of it found him, like her wit was a scent he needed reminding of, as the nurse took herself back down the corridor.

Oran had tried to go in the ambulance with him but Ger had shut that down sharp. After it drove off with Ger inside, Oran stared at the blood still on the floor. When he rang the office he did not lie. He told Brian Junior what had happened. Brian ordered him to take the afternoon off, like he was giving him a raise. Oran drove around, just killing time, but after an hour he told himself it was still Friday and on the way into Burke's he made a token gesture of cocking his head sideways and blowing smoke out. In the gloom of the inn, men stood close to each other and watched the horses on the television on the wall bracket above them. Poles still after the pike in the canal, noted the swollen men, their positions already taken in the wan light, all of them glued to the screen, a miniature tractor beam pulling them in, hopes boxed up into score bets and accas, who d'you have and how much did you have on him. As he came in, he saw Scutch, big Kinnegad head on him, heading to the bar with empties.

Well Howiya, Scutch said.

What's the story?

What'll you have sham?

He made a show of deliberating.

Pint please, he said, like it was a treat. He was set to inhale it. He could hear the lads outside. Gooch had clocked off at four, and started immediately getting lager and Camel Lights into him. Cellophane danced when tapped in the ashtrays. Oran's skin was tight and hot on him. He was finely aware of phones lifted and put down on the barrel before them. The news could arrive at any second. He was chancing his arm staying here, supping. He could see it ahead, the stage whispers of a small town meant for him. He sat smoking, listening to other lads' memories. Gooch was reminding Scutch of his pale flesh.

This cunt never heard of sun cream.

Boys, looking like burnt rashers is the point, Scutch said. Two pints flushed Oran back into order. He wanted it done.

Had an accident in work today.

You shat yourself?

They laughed and he told it quickly. They knew Ger. No one ever had a bad word to say about Ger.

After another swift one he walked to the end of the yard

and rang Michelle. He told her what happened. She said she could get off work early but he told her it was grand. He sucked his fag like a soother. He hung up, headed back in and joined Gooch at the bar. Oran kneaded his diaphragm with the heel of his hand.

I've the bubbleguts, Oran said.

Want some Gaviscon?

You're grand, he said, looking for attention and the bar man came over.

Another three please. On the catch up.

It's your life, the barman said.

The hiss of the tap and the chestnut swirled in the glass. No round dodgers here. Gooch was waving his pint and opinions around and Oran was speeding up. They lowered the drink again and kept a solemn watch on who came in. Gooch was claiming he started ten lads in their year smoking. Scutch was refuting this.

Heard Jamesie got his end away.

There was plenty about.

Scutch stepped neatly behind the bar and poured one himself, the privileges of a true regular.

Sooner or later, you have to talk to them, Scutch said.

Sham that's up to you, Gooch said.

Oran missed his mouth and poured dark stout down his front.

Dribbly balls here, said Gooch, and they all laughed.

Shocking ring sting soon had Oran wincing in the cubicle. He waited for it to subside and checked his phone to find four messages from Michelle. She didn't want to be out tonight. The work was wearing on her. A girl who loved her tunes but these days couldn't listen to the radio on the way home. She had to have silence after the bawling. She could see kids lost in things, no eye contact, fixating on a blank bit of wall, and parents in furious denial. She said she wished more men did the job, that they could use their strength whenever the older ones lost it. Oran always wanted to know who. He was only trying to put a name on who was biting his girlfriend in work but Michelle wouldn't have it, 'they know not what they do' bollix. Far as Oran could see, her whatsapps only pulled a great net of other people's anxieties and problems and babies and no-babies-yet on top of them. The thought insinuated inside himself that they were only doing anything cos they were supposed to be. Like spending Saturday mornings in Kildare Village. They could be doing this online, he'd said last time they went.

You're addicted to shopping too Oran, she'd said back, only all you buy is smokes.

Leave it.

You're shit at shopping. You're always shopping for the same thing.

He'd bared his teeth and followed her round the shops like a toddler. When they got back together after breaking up the first time, his mam had said she knew he would ask Michelle to marry him, because she was the only woman he'd ever spoken about with any nostalgia. No one had ever taken a bad photo of her. She'd laughed at the end of nearly everything he said, made him feel funnier than anyone else ever did. Jamesie, brother of Scutch, came in and confessed his inadequacies. Gooch went in for the kill.

Heard you were shliding around last night, Gooch said.

Now Gooch. Loose lips never served this town or any other.

A code of silence was never the issue, was it?

Sure, Jamesie is a gentleman.

Consenting adults sham, Jamesie said. I don't think I did much.

You wouldn't have to with her—

You've only to show up—

Oran kept slurping as they talked.

Ger was hunched going into the house. He hated being made a fuss over. Dearbh sat him down and got him painkillers.

Night for a takeaway, Dearbh said.

He had been advised to go for soft menu choices, a phrase ugly and new to him. It was Dearbh opened the second bottle, to his vast relief. He savaged eight chicken balls in mechanical succession, no cutting required, as they started in on a crime series she'd saved. They were too hot chomped whole like this and he hopped them around his mouth to get some air in

They're very good at the murders the Swedes, Dearbh said.

Ger offered nothing, enjoying the doughy chew and the warmth of the wine.

And finding out who did it, in fairness, Dearbh said, and looked over at her husband.

Ger reached for his last chicken ball.

Beggared drunk, Oran went to The Seum with the lads: Return to Energizer. This, this here, was the real market square and he took it all in. Shitkickers and lads in leather shoes, young ones strapped into orange dresses and heels, the occasional doomed son drinking the farm away. Over in Foreign Corner the Latvians were as locked as the locals, their corner depleted but still in evidence. The women knew that unlike the rest of them, the lads they've known too long, those lads won't talk. Girls back from college for the weekend slammed shots with their parents and reminded each other of dead babysitters. Oran zeroed in on the metaller in the corner, the one lad in all black with long lank hair, who felt the demons looking into each other after pounding five snakebites. Lad looked like he might have ate his family and this was his last drink before he got out of dodge. By dawn he'd be on the motorway heading for the city, and Oran envied him his options.

He saw Gooch coming towards him. Gooch told him about a terrible smoking area he was in once on a stag in Lahinch, a glass tank looking onto the dance floor, hard to work out who was the fish, the smokers or the dancers. The best man had wanted a no-nonsense two days, just a rake of pints and a massive gaff rented, firing range or go-karts for day two, no brazzers and no messing.

Inside the tunes hit full clamour. Hands aloft, ass everywhere, droplets caught in lamps between wrecked and roaring punters. When the anthem came on everyone leaned in, propping each other up, then wearing the same stare up at the endless menu above them in De Niro's. Oran missed a proper chicken shish on a Saturday night, laughing with the lads at the sign on the wall, Dr Zaytoon holding his stethoscope up to the calories. His stomach growled empty.

Plenty of hepatitis on that Muhammad yeah? Scutch said. Oran looked between Scutch and his kebab, the chilli and garlic sauces swirling to pink.

Nah hang on a fucking second, Oran said.

What you on about?

They've no yoke, the fucking . . . the elephant trunk, Oran said. That the meat comes off.

He leaned over the counter and one of the men behind raised a hand.

Here boys, what youse shaving?

Dead muscle and nails, Scutch said.

You're rotten, Gooch said.

Oran sat back, twirling the plastic fork.

Where's the meat boys? Useless kip.

Watch yourself Howiya, Scutch cautioned.

Bog fucking standard, Oran said.

He hadn't checked his phone in an hour or two. He saw another text from Michelle. She'd sent it a while back. She'd be asleep by now. The most he could hope for was not to wake her up when he got in. If he got into bed stinking of extra garlic sauce, he'd be in the doghouse; if he got in the shower, as she'd once made him, then she'd wake up. He washed his teeth but he still woke her up clambering in. She rolled, twisted and grumbled and it took her hours to get back to sleep.

Monday morning Dearbh drove Ger over to work to have the chat, but not until after the kids were out the door. He wasn't to be in until eleven. Oran was in, earlier than normal, and was rewarded by being told Brian Junior wanted to see him, now he'd spoken to his old man.

We'll call this a verbal warning Oran, Brian said.

Oran knew he should not lose the head in situations like these.

That way we can all move forward, Oran.

Sound that it's we, isn't it?

Excuse me.

It's grand. Doesn't matter.

Thank you, Oran.

They left it there. Oran headed out to finish the job and missed Ger.

Ger felt Dearbh's concern on his back as he walked into

the joinery. When he came in the men stopped talking and he hated that. Brian Senior and Junior were waiting for him in Senior's big office and Brian Junior closed the door over. Inside the son stood to the side. Ger waited for someone to break the quiet. Brian Senior scratched himself in mild concentration. He'd forgotten to wear deodorant and the sour evidence crept inside Ger's nostrils.

How's the claw?

Ger shrugged then rotated it like it wasn't his, a robotic pivot from the wrist.

Grand, Ger said. Not like it does anything.

I feel awful, Ger. And our first accident in how long, Brian?

Twelve years, Dad.

Twelve years, some run. What's most important is you.

Thanks Brian, Ger said.

We'll get you back to your best. Sure, look at me. I took three weeks off last year, took herself to see the grandkids in the States, and it was one of the best things I ever did.

Went nowhere Brian, did I? In the lean years.

You didn't, in fairness to you Ger. Good man. You know we can't be exposed at the minute. We're flying. In a couple of months, you come back and there'll always be something for you here.

Something?

Sure we'll look at it closer to the time.

The silence was thick wallpaper. Brian Junior fingered the rim of his nostril.

We're not going to take it any further than the incident report so? Brian Senior asked him.

Caught where it was too late to have a decent choice, Ger decided then that he wouldn't squeal. It made no odds anyway and he liked Oran.

No, Ger said.

Human error, Brian Senior said, there's none of us perfect. That howiya isn't a bad lad.

The thing we want now is for you to rest up, Ger, Brian Junior said. Few months off.

Right.

Be the makings of you. Good man.

They all shook hands, Ger using his left hand, everyone making jokes about getting used to it.

Oran sent Ger a text asking how he was getting on. Ger sent him the thumbs up, then jabbed out a response, said he was as much use as a chocolate teapot. Oran sent him the crying laugh back.

In work Oran got stuck with a new lad, younger and thicker than him. Ozzo, a child of twenty-three years old. Oran found himself less funny: he was no craic like this, the mentor role wasn't him. It was like he was taking someone on work experience. Oran reluctantly clued up on how his job had changed and what he was supposed to do, mostly mind this little sap who'd barely got his safety pass.

They told Ger they would operate and try to reattach it. It was just there, now it wasn't. He had a secret that nobody else needed, that it should have been a lot worse. He flung himself at productivity, up as early as ever, working out what he could do, manoeuvring sizzling sausages around a pan, filling the kitchen with their aroma and learning the hard way that his son doesn't want a fry on a Wednesday morning.

I'd smell of dead pig for the rest of the day, Jase said. You trying to have me bullied?

o

It was dead quiet after they left for school. Ger methodically cleared the plate of six sausages himself. The afternoons muddled and stretched. He tried to read the newspaper. He went off music. He was stuck in the house and mangled with it.

That Friday Oran and Michelle were out in Dudek's, the Italian run by a Polish couple. They had just sat down when Kara and Dean came in. Here we go, Oran thought, these fucking two. They were definitely going on holiday, or just back: hard to tell when Kara's tan was always rich and perfect. Kara's sister had a make-up line, sixty thousand followers and free holidays. Michelle had caught him once, looking at Kara's pole-dancing profile on his phone, while he was supposed to be ordering a takeaway.

That giving you ideas?

Fuck off.

Wondering what she looks like on the pole, are you?

Well, I wasn't wondering what he fucking looks like on it. Michelle had laughed, that little yelp that he was hearing less and less.

Dean fucking twerking away, he'd said and they'd both laughed. Now Michelle beckoned the smiling pair over and he wanted to kill her for it. Oran knew as they came over that the dogs of her own envy would be at the table by the time they left.

How's things? Michelle asked them.

Things are engaged! Kara shouted and showed them the ring, a glittering cut boulder.

You're getting an exclusive, Dean said.

Can we get youse a round? Oran asked.

No, it's on us. We insist.

Kara and Dean left them, Dean's hand roving from her lower

back to her ass. Michelle insisted on sending them over a pair of congratulatory espresso martinis.

When they never pay for their own anyway? Fucking joke.

It's two drinks, Oran. It won't cost you the fucking ring. They each ordered the steak, and had the craic, until the other two left early. They'd some neck, going round town, fucking up other people's Friday nights. Michelle went home but Oran said he'd find the lads for a few and he found The Seum and Eloise, catching his eye and flicking her hair. Oran thought that she must know he was thinking bout fucking her. There were birds who were pretty but they weren't hot. Eloise was new and fuckable. Deafening shit rising over the speakers and the Rihanna wasn't helping his horn. She was all suggestion to him, all smirk and welcome, danger signs and green lights. She sashayed over and slowed in front of him.

Eloise is out.

Here I am.

They rolled with the shoulders of the crowd.

Out for the night?

With any luck, she said.

They were briefly pressed into each other. She dropped her hand to his fly and through the rough denim he felt his cock rise with her fingers. She was sliding her grin towards him.

You should get that seen to, Eloise said.

A glass smashed. A wildfire of woos spread out through the crowd. The eyebrows climbed her face. He lent her a crack of his smile as his spidered fingers raised pints.

For the troops, he said.

See you later.

With his skill lost, the weeks shrank the house on Ger. Getting the slow lift through Hell, the scratch. He felt like a well-meaning sub-species, like Dearbh had under kind sufferance taken this lame oaf into her home. He sensed a giant pressing down on the town, no badness in the giant, just heavy, making it hard to look up at the day. He rolled over, a grumpy whale on a cotton beach, but sleep would not come. He looked into room after room during the day. It all felt damp and crushed. He never knew how much talk radio she listened to, a constant chattering, scorpions in his head. Health is freedom, they said, as the kitchen windows speckled with the next shower. Too much news was no use to anyone. The dimensions of a day had changed on him, going round prideless and wrecked from doing nothing. He tried to wash the dishes, awkward, a plate held in his armpit, until she relieved him of that too. Mondays he went with her to Aldi. He couldn't say he'd anything better on. After it had rained, there was no colour on the roads, just mirrory silver blank. He began to obsess over other people's hands. He watched his daughter's deft typing. Maeve did not look up from her screen as she deadpanned it into him.

It's not your whole hand Dad.

He used to sleep like a log. He was grateful for the podcasts now he couldn't. He liked the Fall of Civilizations, appreciated the soft chat about places far away and long ago, three hours at a time on Byzantium. He was listening to one on the Greenland Vikings when Jase came home one night stocious, clattering around outside, his legs not behaving themselves, then a wet splash of sick onto plants and gravel. He could be heard fumbling with the key but Ger was up as Dearbh mumbled with rubbery lips into the pillow. He patiently guided his son indoors, whispering at him not to wake the house and he got him water and put him to bed.

Dearbh went to Seafield with Elaine for the weekend.

Good enough for the Leinster team, Ger said to her, have at it. Twelve county army, they were mad on selling that now, big pink Tadhg Furlong hitting tyres in the ads. Left to fend for himself, Ger walked down to De Niro's for dinner but he saw a bouncer deliver a crossarm against some young fella's neckpipe and he turned tail and ate two bowls of cereal at home.

So, I can only emphasize again the benefits of moist wound healing and hydrocolloid dressings for the best possible recovery.

Ger's hand was mostly itchy gristle, an angry hiving just below the surface. He was shown how to gently tap the end of the finger daily and massage it to help desensitize it. The way they kept calling it his finger got to him: if his finger was all there, he'd be in work. Nerve damage can take up to a year to get better, he was told, so he began slowly climbing the mountain of health goals, coaxing his finger back. Dearbh bought him rosehip oil. She drove them everywhere now, and life was parking. Inside the Aldi he looked at the cheap meat while she stocked up on hummus, rashers and multipacks of pizzas. She suggested he check out the middle aisle. He was looking at the plastic tools, Fisher-Price stuff, when he heard a voice he knew from parent–teacher meetings, looked up and saw its owner approaching with a blizzard of kids belting each other. He scrambled away and nearly dove into the frozen turkeys to get his head down. Crouched, he listened as his wife was filled in on the events in the lounge of Fagan's the night previous.

Ah they're feral, one worse than the next.

Mulcahy was like a tinker over it, the woman said.

Ger kept his head in the freezer. He said nothing on the way home. She looked amused in the car.

What?

How was that for you? Dearbh asked.

He tried to show some faint optimism but he wasn't selling it.

That bad?

He pulled at the fat of his lip as he considered it.

It's another country, he said.

Go easy, Dearbh kept saying when it was just the two of them. After another night and another hour of murder scenes in the snow, Ger made to get off the couch.

You're not opening another bottle, Dearbh said.

He sat back down. He felt the blinkers were on, all the colour sucked out of it, the point of things dulled and faded. He took it to bed.

Dearbh's sister dropped in after lunch. She would talk the hind legs off Dearbh and Ger's suspicion was nobody ever turned Linda's volume down years ago, and it was out of control now. He stayed up in the bedroom like a rat while they snapped Weight Watchers points back and forth below before Linda roared up for him. Ger did not respond.

Having his siesta, Linda said. A grown man sleeping in the middle of the day.

He's not actually, Linda, it's the new headphones. Noise cancelling.

A vague, unshruggable thing hung on him. The need of a piss had him heading for the bathroom and his bulk on the landing sent a giveaway creak down, alerting them to his presence. He listened to his wife lie for him.

You hiding up there like the Jew in the attic? Linda shouted.

Elaine, what kind of person worries about Jews in attics? Dearbh shot back.

He nearly blushed at her defence of him. He would not surface. He would not answer their questions.

Oran was parked outside Ozzo's mam's gaff and it was no help to his temperament. Ozzo was always late, and Oran was waiting on him again. Waiting on the slightest indiscretion. Eventually he came out, Oran thinking how much Ger would get some craic out of the kid's mullet as he slouched towards the van. They got on the road.

Oran himself was strictly under the gaze of Brian Junior since the accident. Junior must smirk in his sleep, he thought. Thinking back to Canada as he drove them to work. Making so much cash you couldn't spend it all but you could have a lash at it and watching the new Hardy Bucks when you got in. They'd repeated the best lines at each other for years after: if there was work in the bed you'd sleep on the floor. Ozzo spent lunch swiping until Oran barked at him to turn the sounds off.

Pure demon scratch and Ger climbed the stairs for some privacy, for what he already knew and in the bedroom he unpeeled the stinking wraps. He considered the raw stub of it, the black gnarled end of it sorry looking. It didn't take. Sitting on their bed he knew this long before he told anyone. He wanted to go to seed. He couldn't bring himself to call the doctor that night. He got under the covers and put his ears in podcasts before Dearbh came up.

In the morning he rang first thing and an hour later Ger sat in front of the doctor, who was closer in age to Jase than himself, dressed in maroon slacks.

I'm afraid I don't have good news for you, Gerard.
The doctor went on but Ger had stopped listening. It was just

static pouring out the doctor's mouth. He felt he should not have it then.

Just, just stick it in the bin there, Ger said.

Are you sure?

I am thanks. I won't miss it now.

The young doctor hesitated, holding it, hanging there. Ger looked at it, a dirty little worm.

Do I need to do it for you?

No, no. Sorry.

Finally, it was disposed of.

Thank you, Ger said.

Dearbh tried to push down his sullen silence, chatting on while he stared out the window. The light packed it in at half four and the townlands would stay low across the late hours. Jase had gone vegan for Lent.

More work for your mother, Ger said.

At dinner the kids talked about Billie Eilish while Ger tried to coax his left hand into twisting some spag bol onto the fork, with no success: the pasta slapped back on the plate and spat sauce on his shirt.

She's depressed a lot, Jason said solemnly.

It's her mental health, Maeve said.

Ger saw the finger in his sleep. The missing end did not want to leave his dreams.

Rumours were the currency of the town and it was a rumour that took Oran down on a sad sack Sunday. He'd come in the door and dropped his keys on the side table. He heard the thin tinkling of wine glasses in the kitchen, before he heard Michelle's voice, but not like normal. Her tone was all wrong.

That you?

Yeah, he said. Who else would it be?

She spoke as he entered the kitchen.

Thought it might be Eloise Houlihan, she said then.

The fear lashed into him. Her face was twitching, little spasms now she'd said it, now they were here. He fixed his eyes to their shit imitation floor.

You said it. All them celebrities that can't stop riding any gash with a pulse. You said it.

He remembered saying it.

All Jay-Z had to do was fuck Beyoncé. I remember loving you for that. You got it then Oran. When did you stop getting it? Her voice quavered and she looked wounded and confused.

I'm a joke for young ones, the fucking teenagers in Aldi. Eloise and that howiya, they said.

His mouth dropped slack and open.

I didn't even finish the shopping. Left it all in the trolley. One of them bitches will have to put it all back now . . .

He understood he had to let her finish.

Then I was a mess in the car park. You made a mess out of me.

That started her going, wracked her chest.

What's that Oran? What's she?

Nothing. She's nothing.

Why d'you need a cover version of me?

Ah hang on.

What the fuck are you?

Fuck off.

Climbing down into someone else's bed.

What d'you want me to say?

I don't want you to say anything. You've fucking said it all, Oran, that's the point. And you didn't say it with your mouth. But we're a bit past that now, aren't we?

He didn't answer. He wasn't sure if it was a question.

Aren't we?

Yeah. We are.

What are we?

She was pulling her work moves on him, repeating shit, and he had to stand there and take it.

We're a bit past that.

Thank you, Oran. Now take that busy little phone out and ring your mates. Or her.

He looked up in shock.

I don't care to be honest with you, she said. You're not snoring here tonight.

She was trembling. He crashed into disgust with himself, at what he'd done to her face, creased and raw and small.

I don't know what to do. Who do I ring? Not my fella. My mam? Tell her she was right?

Then she turned to the kitchen counter and reefed open the cutlery drawer. She grabbed a fork and stabbed herself in the abdomen. She made a terrible sound and doubled over and did it again, her eyes clamped closed, tears streaming as Oran leapt in. She tried to get him with it and he grabbed her wrist with one hand and wrested it off her with the other and fucked it across the room and they broke apart. The venom quiet after. She'd tested herself enough, upset herself at the scene, swallowing tears like she might choke on them, and all Oran knew was that he wasn't allowed get closer to her, that this was now denied to him. She shrank against the counter.

Thought you could cop on, she said.

Come on Michelle.

You can't, can you. Incapable.

Ah fuck off Michelle—

You boring fucking prick.

He was snared for something he almost did. He had fucked

up before and got away with them. He had never really fucked
Eloise Houlihan. Not for want of trying. It had been a late one,
months back, everyone bananas after The Seum. Fluorescents
fluttered and sprang bright when they'd landed in Scutch's
garage with the pool table. After Gooch ripped the cloth of
the table with the cue, they'd all left the room until it was just
Oran and Eloise, her back to the wall, her lips petulant. They
were on each other fast, her tongue fat and insistent, until
they were in the side room on the futon. But when he finally
got what he wanted that night he could do nothing with it.
He couldn't find any steel in him. He thought her sigh didn't
need to be that loud. She got off him and he slid out, defeated.

Whiskey dick, is it?

Sorry.

Fucking eight-pint noncock, more like.

She got off the bed and dressed and that took forever. He
stared at the ceiling.

Fuck sake. Pining for my pussy in public and now you're
no fucking use.

He walked home after, anything to not listen to the same taxi
drivers as every night.

Back in this kitchen aftermath, Michelle looked emptied
in front of him, steadying herself by the counter, but he knew
all he could do was leave.

Ger was hardly drinking raw eggs at dawn but one morning
when he couldn't sleep he got up, busy against the blue and
made himself a big coffee and got out early, no more lying
awake looking at the same nothing, no more feeling like a
freak at half five. He closed the front door. The air was cold
and clear on his face. Everything was still coated in indigo and
he started at a good clip. The day revealed itself and he liked
the quiet, the morning rising with the birds. He walked for

two hours plus. He found honest sweat in the roads, salt up in his eyes, remembering the Davy Fitz story he loved. When Davy first got on the senior panel, Leo Doyle from Bodyke was his competition between the sticks. Doyle was working in Shannon so Davy would be up, cycling in the dark to a spot he knew, where he'd stretch and as the dawn chorus began, he'd start, pucking the sliotar off the wall, the only sound for miles around, until Doyle's car approached. Davy never looked up as Doyle drove past him, after he'd let Doyle know just who was outworking him. Davy would cycle home after, whistling to himself, happy to be stuck in Doyle's head. Ger felt beams inside him, fresh sweat bright on him as others shivered. This would be him, aching with happy calves. He'd go after it like Davy Fitz and the town could be Doyle.

The night Michelle threw him out, Oran nearly went to Dublin, but he ended up in Furlong's.

Fair balls, Scutch said, when Oran set down the pints.

What happened you? Gooch asked.

Don't start.

Doghoused? You bold boy. Your badness caught up with you.

Karma sham, counselled Scutch. It's an unholy cunt.

He didn't need Scutch telling him a thing. He slagged him back and got out to the smoking area for more poison. The ancient cleaner was in the corner, tapping her smoke. He had two and so did she. He had to listen to them all around. He got sludged there in Furlong's, rounds flying and all of them steaming, when Dean had joined them, mates with the boys since school, and it didn't take long for Dean to start telling them about all the plates he was spinning, how he could barely find enough people for the work, how he'd take a few game chimpanzees at this rate. Oran's ears pricked up and he leaned across the table.

Chimpanzees eat their own shite, Scutch said.

Oran fought for clarity in all the shouting, but Dean was only having the one and he had his jacket on, making for the door. Oran got after him. He put himself in front of Dean, nearly shouldered him doing it. Dean backed up, scowling, but Oran stood him up: he still looked like he boxed even if he stopped at twelve. Dean had never boxed.

All good Oran?

C'mere, there a job going?

Could be.

I have the man for it.

A lot of men would be glad of this job.

They won't be as good as the man I have for you, Ger.

Dean mulled it.

Herself wants a fitted kitchen, Dean said.

Yeah?

You do kitchens.

I do, yeah.

Works for everyone so.

Deal.

Get on to me next week.

Sound.

Dean nodded and pushed on. Oran nearly texted Ger on the spot, but he was trying not to always go with the first thought he had.

Ger heard what people were saying: Dearbh told him. She was mad for the gossip, like that was what she really went shopping for, putting tales in her trolley along with the four-euro chickens. He felt sorry for Michelle. He didn't know her, more she was someone to ask about. You got to dance with who you came with. It was a shame to him. His sister, late one night, once told him Eloise and her friend came in late and woke her up, shouting about serving cunt. The phrase stopped him and stuck on him. He was thinking about it the rest of the weekend and had to deflect when Dearbh caught him staring at her on the couch and asked him what was up with him. That was the lad's problem. Oran couldn't hack leaving a world where young ones served cunt and thinking like that could only get you in trouble.

On the Monday Oran got onto him and they got a coffee the next Saturday and walked over the horse bridge, the stone seat long worn shiny by the arses of unemployed men.

How's the form? Ger asked.

Thriving, Oran said, rolling his eyes.

Same as meself.

You're missed in there.

Ah. I miss myself, Ger said.

At the crumbled castle they turned and walked along the riverbank.

You're looking well, Oran said.

I never stopped moving son.

Oran nodded but kept his mouth shut.

Eloise they're saying, Ger said.

Something like that.

Ah lad. That's my niece.

Wasn't you I was thinking of.

Wasn't Michelle either.

Oran stared at the mud under the bench before he spoke.

Here, you're not looking for work are you?

You moved into Recruiting?

Just this once.

The wind bit into them.

In the Woodie's out by the Long Mile. A CSA.

A what? Ger asked.

Customer service assistant. Aul ones come in, ask where the light bulbs are.

Right.

You tell them. I know the lad who's manager there. Piece of piss.

OK. Sure, see what you can do.

It's a handy one.

Fuck off, you.

No, I didn't mean it like that. Sorry.

Ger narrowed his eyes but saw that Oran didn't mean it. He really didn't.

Not taking the piss. I'm not that smart, Oran said.

They said they'd meet up for a drink, though both knew it was just a thing to say. Oran took his phone out to send on the number, but Ger told him later on would be grand and Oran put his phone away. Ger took off before Oran. He had to see his physio. The exercises the physio gave Ger lent him a new kind of faith. He liked the physio: he looked like a tennis player and Ger liked getting studied, given little physical trials he was able for, and encouraged after. Dearbh slagged him, said he thought he was an Olympian now.

Oran started hiding out in Scutch's while Michelle packed up, her mam helping. He wasn't there so no drama, none of her dad, waiting at the door of the car, refusing to come in or talk to him. Most things left from the break-up went with her but she forgot a few. Her leggings and knickers he shoved down the back of his old sports bag behind Scutch's sofa.

o

Ger waited to tell Dearbh until after she'd parked. She hugged him as they sat outside the dusking house and they stayed wrapped around each other and she made a satisfied sound as he inhaled the warm kind smell of her.

You deserve that.

It's a job for a kid.

Stop it.

She squeezed his hand and they kissed.

You been like a dog in the vet, with your cone of shame, she said.

Dearbh reached across and unzipped her husband's fly.

Something else you can't do yourself, she said, grinning as she tucked her hair back and his breath rose and she lowered her open mouth onto him. That night in bed he curled up around her. She held him. He nuzzled into her, no podcast and no headphones, and he fell asleep straight after.

Oran sent on Dean's number and Ger gave him a ring. They set up an interview and the interview was grand, barely an interview at all. The next week he was back in a team. The team was a real mix, the kids were bored but he got on with Susan, closer to his own age, and she had the measure of the rest of them and they had good craic together as he learned the ropes. The months turned and Ger's hand healed up and he flexed it and it let him hold things again and drive himself home. Gradually the monkey climbed back down off his back and he never knew it was a gorilla until it was gone.

Oran did his penance, his Saturdays spent on his knees in Dean and Kara's, finishing off their dream kitchen. Dean was only allowed to air kiss Kara so he wouldn't mess up her look, and he went out for his 10k as Kara sashayed her hole before Oran, every move a pose as she took shots for the gram, fifty pouting options for every one posted. His mind flew to fantasies, scenarios filled with Kara bent over the sink, begging for more. When Dean came back panting and sweaty, Oran looked up from the floor and realized even Dean wasn't fucking her. He was just taking photos to get other lads thinking about fucking her. Dean was only a photographer for a minor celebrity. Oran went to their jacks and came shuddering into their porcelain sink.

He ended up staying in Casa Scutch for a while, Kung Po chicken and PS3 on a Tuesday and the first few weeks were class. They played FIFA matches in real time like the old days, ninety minutes a go. Some nights late, with the cans shook empty and the football cursed, Oran would think what to say to her, thoughts that came only at times he couldn't do anything with them, his cartwheeling brain on his pillow. His last thought that night and many nights after was that he could drive out to her parents' gaff. Declare some shit. Win her back. What if you learn it all but by the time you have it you've no one for it.

Evenings spoiled easy after. No arms came around him that night, tossing and turning in the box room. No curls came to rest on his chest. Only the muck of what he'd done. Everything he missed, a fuzzy kaleidoscope of her, only the best bits of her, never boring and never wrong and he couldn't miss her more. He ran through all the body parts he had rejected them for, cycling and rotating through them, all their parts on dark loop, the hang of a belly, the fat of an arm, the droop of a tit and he could make a monster from them now.

CRISPY BITS

If I could, I'd climb between your ribs and cover your heart with my mouth.

Darragh had said it to Hannah in this bed they would never share again. She tried to remember that morning. It had been this year, only months ago, the end of January. He'd looked surprised when he'd said it, which made two of them. He'd probably still been wired at the time but she'd hugged him into her like it was true, or she wanted to make it true. She'd probably still been wired herself. She guessed she'd thought they'd live together, come home and find each other in the evening, but now they never would. She wouldn't remind him of any of that now. The bells of Christchurch rang out beyond the window, a sharp Sunday in May. They were close enough to see some of the other in the dark pools of their pupils. How had they moved from that spellbound warmth to the muttered awful of whatever this was, mumbled half sentences falling to inevitable. He'd brought them to this, he set the trap but it was up to her to put the animal down. She hated him for that and she hated that they were in his place.

We don't have a hope, do we? she said.

He shook his head slowly, like he hadn't started it. Once he'd yielded to doubt there was no way back. She knew all this. She'd learned the hard way before. She had hoped he was past it, or she was past lads like this. Lads didn't trust themselves, then they didn't trust who they faced, then they broke it and left you with the pieces. She clawed at all the moments they were about to scrub away. They each saw what shone most, what they would each miss most in the months to come, before they were lost to each other.

It wasn't the first week where the pain lived. That was booze and food and more food and home for the weekend. It was after that hollowed you out, when you've to go back to less than before, the tundra of midweek and all your extra evenings.

Hannah mined through the next week, trying to see past being crushed and quaked by it all. She installed an app she said she'd never use. She kept her phone off her desk and out of sight but by night she was curled up in bed, flicking past their best faces. The ease of dismissal. She wondered when being single had turned apocalyptic. The faces and decisions sunk in the past. The good ones claimed by now.

It hit giddy summer, the sky showboating in royal blue and Hannah searched for Kate on the canal. She found her friend, cross-legged and frowning at the crowds.

Hey. You got a spot, Hannah said.

Kate slowly eyed others on the deck.

Locals only would be nice, said Kate, who had lived nearby for three years.

Hannah said nothing, let her have it.

Sorry I'm late, she said.

You're grand, Kate said, offering her a can. Don't I have the swans for company?

That's not company, Hannah said, that's a threat.

She scowled at the sinuous mob on the muddy bank a few feet away, black nothing in their eyes.

Sinister pricks.

Can't even eat them.

Kate stared off into the water.

I reckon all the disappeared lads, yeah? On the posters.

What bout them? Hannah asked.

Maybe it's the swans, Kate said. The swans disappeared them.

Wouldn't put anything past them, Hannah said.

The canal stopped talking to watch a man of sixty move along the glinting water on a paddle board. On the front of the board a collie sat like a sphinx.

The amount that do disappear, Hannah said. People go missing all the time. More than we ever talk about. Every lamp post could be someone lost.

Hannah shivered as she ashed the can. It turned on you when the sun went in and the shank of cold left you stark in the shadows.

Darragh had his laptop and whatsapp synced so he got the message twice in quick succession, but it was not who he wanted. It was Gav. His mate's name and message sprang up in the corner of his screen.

– Scoops tomorrow? I'm gasping.

For once Darragh was first and early for him. He picked a craft beer like he'd pick a horse: back anything with a good name and plenty of go. He sipped the tangy pint and read the paper on his phone. He scrolled through the disasters. He was grateful for the World Cup to begin. The first goal scorers, the podcasts and the Colombian left backs, a thousand details to get lost in. They wouldn't be going here after Thursday, this place had no interest in showing matches and they were about to come thick and fast. Gav took World Cups very seriously – four years ago, he'd found himself dumped before the group stages were over.

Gav arrived and the pints rolled in. They picked salty peanuts from a bed of flashing foil and mulled over the fortunes of the summer to come. Gav sluiced his pint down and took in the room.

I notice when someone's my age in here, he said.

A bored girl glided out from behind the bar and moved around the tables. Gav nudged Darragh.

Watch this shit, he said.

The girl stopped and examined a vintage lamp at a nearby table. She adjusted it, precise as an optician, but left the fringed lampshade lopsided and walked away. Darragh turned to Gav, appalled.

Did that just happen?

I know, Gav said. They're *supposed* to be off.

Mother of fuck.

The girl approached another table. Again, she leaned in and again she angled the lampshade carefully askew, wronged it by twenty degrees. As she drew herself back up to check her handiwork, she caught them staring. Scolded, they flung their looks away.

We've seen something we shouldn't, Gav said.

Arsehole bars followed us home, Darragh said

Blame London.

Every chance I get. Won't be any decent barmen soon, just beards on legs.

This place never had a chance.

Ah there was no gun to our head, Darragh said.

They went quiet, lifted pints to faces, poured it in.

Any other craic? Gav asked him.

Nah, Darragh said.

He'd tell Gav later, but three hours and five pints later he hadn't. He was thinking that he should have left Gav to it but it was a bit late now. He'd gone to the slaughter with him and now they stood dumb in the kebab shop, the fumes rising off them, Gav in bezerker mode and texting as they ate, trying to pull a session out of his phone. Darragh forked shaved meat into his mouth as Gav threw names out.

What about Kev? Always heads at his.

You're persona non grata there.

Oh yeah.

Gav didn't need reminding why invites to Kev's had not been forthcoming ever since Gav was overheard calling Kev's obese flatmate the Trippopotamus.

We used to know where to go, Gav muttered.

No, we didn't, Darragh said, we just got lost better.

They ended up getting two bottles of wine from the Indian. By the time Darragh made for home the street sweepers were out, grumbling up the road, herding the rubbish that whipped past him in the bitter dawn.

Hannah knew she was scratchy in work. She checked herself: if she was going to snap at every sunny co-worker younger than her, she would have to commit to snapping at all of them and their stupid terms, fur babies and breakfast margies. This was the price of employment in a start-up. At thirty-one she was the old crone of the office. Come the weekend, she was glad to meet up with Kate and the girls. She tried to listen to her friends and keep her chin up out of her own poxy stew.

Even the word is horrible, Tríona said.

Shmear, repeated Kate, savouring the reaction round the table.

Stop saying shmear. It's worse, Tríona said.

Why's it worse? asked Kate.

Smear's not the worst, Hannah said.

Shhhhhmear.

Scrape is the worst.

Shcraped out of it, Kate said, and they sent disgusted laughs skyward.

Anyway, you wouldn't know whose you'd get back, Hannah said. Lucky dip.

Later, when it was just the two of them sunk into the night, Kate copped it fast.

What happened? she asked Hannah.

Hannah considered feigning ignorance. She looked at her oldest friend again and knew it pointless.

How did you know?

Ah it's hardly subtle, hun. You might as well turn up at his office in the morning, drenched in blood and gin, roaring I'm grand at him, just as he's swiping his laminate.

The tournament went into the knockouts, when there's more games gone than to come. He'd been working for a betting giant for a few years, and still wished he was in the marketing department, talking shite over a slab, throwing round puns, shovelling coal for the great green god of banter. The weird hours at work were a wind-up and it was only getting busier but he had days to take off or he'd lose them so he joined the evening trudge home and mulled this as town cleared out. He realized he still had her earphones in his pocket, loaned for a trip to the shops when the hunger pangs had them both and he had gone on a mission to the deli counter. He had fast-fading things in his fridge that needed cooking but he crossed the cobbles of Castle Street so he could pass Burdock's and inhale its hot hug of fat. He wondered if you could walk in and just get the crispy bits without the brick of chips. The harsh-lit aisles of Tesco Express felt full of food for two and he walked home along the winding spine of the South Circular, a Sale Agreed sign on every other house.

When he let himself in, the mat was covered in junk, snack box deals on chipper flyers and hungry, glossy numbers from estate agents asking if they were Thinking of Selling? The house was full of jobs half done, ripe bins and escalating laundry. He hid his wounds badly.

Hannah and Kate were Out. They sat out the back of a bouncing bank holiday Sugar Club, amped up on each other's company. Kate had the hop on her by two cocktails, her spleen fuelled by rum. Hannah loved her in this mood; she saw less of it these days. They watched the dancers inside every time the security-hinged door swung open to let smokers out. A low growl came from Kate. Her lips barely moved as she kept her eyes on the interior.

I would pull the dreads off him, said Kate and Hannah followed her look. All the lads were doing the white-boy head snap, except for one, the matted snakes swaying from his crown and down his back, his body open to lower frequencies. The door shut again and their view was lost.

I would be his dog on a string, Kate said.

The way you're looking at him, you are.

Dunno what you're talking bout, babe.

I'll get you a restraining order. Or a bucket.

Relax. Just cos I've ordered doesn't mean I can't look at the menu.

Maybe you want what you can't have, Hannah thought, watching her friend's thirsty looks. Hannah liked Neal, Kate's fiancé, but he was definitely more Lynx Africa than Afrobeat. Neal had almost definitely seen dreadlocks, Hannah reckoned, most likely on the cover of his Legend CD. Their talk slowly wound round to Darragh and Kate wasn't having it.

I don't want to say anything that may be held against me later, Kate said.

Don't worry, said Hannah. We're done.

OK, I'll go in so. Like he was grand. Sound, easy on the eye, but . . . reptilian.

Reptilian?

Yeah. Ahh, not just him. All these cold-blooded lads and we're supposed to warm them up.

Hannah laughed despite herself.

Fuck it. Ain't nobody got time for that, Kate said.

We don't have the sun for it either, Hannah said.

And y'know what? Fuck mutual. It's never been mutual. They don't start mutual do they? Someone leaps, someone asks, or swipes. Someone acts. And they sure as fuck don't end on mutual either. That's the lie we build it all on. Mutual, Kate declared, slurping her mojito loudly through her straw for punctuation, mutual is bollix.

Hannah sighed and rested her head on her friend's shoulder. She'd have loved to stay there. Eventually she stood and went in, everyone a foot taller and armed with elbows and bomber jackets. A few bodies over she saw the lad with dreadlocks they'd been perving on. He looked spoken for, a Spanish girl grinding up on him, looking back up at him as they moved together. The bar was a wall of bodies before her, thirsty lads knocking off each other. She'd given up on being tall years ago but tonight took too many size twelves planted on her toes. Finally, the crowd parted and she slid in and placed her wrist on the bar. Sticky, the bar clung back. She frowned, yanked her hand away and felt she was being watched. She turned to a new face. His stubbled jaw held some silver. He looked fun.

Here, he said.

He passed her a fat stack of napkins. She wiped her wrist with care, feeling his attention hot on her.

Thanks, she leaned in, shouting over the bass and racket.

What's the story? he asked.

All of it?

Yeah?

No story. I was only hatched tonight.

Ah that's two of us so.

Crystalline vocals froze around them and they each got served. They stepped out of it together and the crush relaxed away from the bar.

You been christened yet? she asked.

Aaron.

Hannah. Come on you can meet Kate.

Hannah smiled on the twist of her heel. Back at the table, Kate grinned, watched the two of them, sucked her drink down to the slush and made herself scarce. Aaron got them in and over the next hour they each dropped a reference to their exes and the night glowed with dizzy hope.

Is another drink thick? she asked him and he shrugged back in a way she noted.

Maybe tomorrow, he said. Right now it's a fucking great idea.

They kissed, a lovely drunko buzz, all inhale and surge as they pulled into each other. After soft slipped minutes she let herself down from up on her toes. She touched her chin, convinced it was raw and flushed pink.

Sorry. It's scratchy. Your beard.

Pain in the hole shaving.

He caught her look coming and her mouth opening.

I'm not moaning, he scrambled. I'll live with shaving the face.

Aren't you the best buachaill?

She watched his face flicker, eager and blinking, and the rum felt firm and certain in her.

You don't have a clue how much you don't have a clue, she said.

Say again?

D'you think biology is misogynist? she asked.

I . . . I hadn't thought bout it like that.

She was lit up watching the cogs turn.

What d'you reckon? he asked.

She thought his question was a start. They shimmered before each other then, in the inkling this might work. Two drinks fuzzier she blurted it out.

I'm just out of something. I just, I want to say that and I want you to hear it.

OK. I hear you.

Just, it's complicated, yeah?

Yeah. I mean you're right. Maybe . . .

Maybe? she asked.

Maybe it's all complicated.

Mad complicated.

Maybe it's mad simple.

And they kissed again and it wasn't Monday yet.

It was a school night and Darragh had crowded tabs open on pornhub. He was familiar with a lot of the faces and their stuffed tits, though he didn't get all this incest shit. You should have to go looking for that, he reckoned, but maybe everyone had run out of everything wrong. He watched a woman pretend to be picked up by laughing men in a jeep. With his other hand he scrubbed along until she was getting fucked, screaming hysterically, Hit It Harder in gnarled script across her belly as she howled and bucked. He was close when Hannah's name appeared at the top right of the screen, beside the shaking flesh.

– Hey

He leapt and gripped himself hard. He stopped but the screaming kept playing in his ears.

Finally he muted it. The room was silent. The message faded off. He did nothing for a minute. Eventually he tucked himself back into his boxers and fumbled the buttons into place and unplugged her earphones. It was five weeks since they'd split.

– I've a pair of tickets to Japandroids but I can't go, if you want them?

It was him who had put her onto them in the first place. He'd planned to get a pair himself and that way gently strong-arm one of the lads into going but they'd sold out fast.

– Love to go yeah. Happy to take the two of them.

– Deadly.

– D'you want to meet up after work?

– I can't. Mental this week. Sorry.

He saw she was still typing so he let her type.

– I'll email them to you.

– OK. Thanks.

The weeks before a gig he listened to nothing else but the band he was going to see and afterwards he wouldn't listen for months. That night he was rushing after work, trying to get in and out the door in half an hour. He opened a can and showered and shaved and stuck on the only things in his wardrobe he liked and printed the tickets off and fired the can into the recycling and shoved the tickets in his pocket and hurried into town.

Cranes hung above and the concrete was rising in Blackpitts. He thought of his friends' gaffs as a kid, when he knew exactly the smell and the pets and he didn't know the smell of his own gaff now and he didn't want to either.

The scalpers hung outside the Olympia and he waited for Gav. He lit up and drew smoke into his lungs, watching everyone who went by. The squat men all knew each other and hawked tickets, shouting buying or selling. A homeless man approached Darragh, the man's eyes hiding from the focused world and the health sucked out of his skin.

D'you have a smoke? the man asked.

D'you want to roll one?

You do it, you don't know where my hands have been.
He held up his calloused hands, the nails caked with filth.

Only messing. Nowhere exciting. See him?
They looked across the road at a dumpster and just past it where some cardboard shifted and a head briefly appeared and disappeared just as fast. Darragh started rolling for him.

Gives rest of us a bad name, the man said. Aul one last week, he sees her with a fat envelope, a down payment, on her way to the credit union. Slapped her round and left her on the deck.
Darragh nodded along, unsure what he could add to the conversation.

He's not sick. Prick.
Darragh kept an eye on the street. She could arrive any time. He glanced back to the man, who was still staring ahead with eyes narrowed.

If you're sick, the man said, go home and lie down in your flat, yeah?

Darragh licked and folded the skin and passed the smoke to the man.

Thanks buddy, god bless.

Good luck, Darragh said, and nearly died after. What the fuck was that, good luck. He kept running through all the other shocking options, all the countless ways he could have been wrong – have a good one, take care, mind yourself – while he waited for Gav.

Cold dread coursed through her the second she copped it. She'd sent Darragh their two tickets by mistake: the two under Aaron's name. Now Darragh had the ones Aaron had bought, not the ones she'd bought. She stared at the bolted ceiling of the bus. No takebacks. She whipped around in her seat, trapped and harried by it. She didn't know she was knocking the seat in front of her with her knee until the woman in front of her turned around and let her know. She said sorry a bunch of times and looked out the window and tried not to catch her own reflection. Nothing she could do now. She made herself late, texted Aaron her apologies, got off the bus early and walked the rest of the way to calm herself down.

The bar was three deep in Brogan's and Gav urged him out the back and into the alley amongst the stacked kegs for their ritual smoke. Darragh handed Gav the second ticket. Gav stared at the information on it. Then they both did, Darragh looking over his mate's shoulder.

That's him so, Gav said.

Name doesn't help, Darragh said.

Gav's smoke got in his face as he looked back.

What, Gav said, you were hoping the lad's surname was Cromwell?

Something like that, Darragh said and folded his ticket and stuck it in his pocket.

So, she's not coming? Gav asked.

Dunno, Darragh said, but he was head up and scanning about as he said it.

He's not anyway, Gav said.

Yeah. Dunno.

They went into the crimson and gilded old theatre and down the hard sloped floor to the rotunda bar, the heat pressing in as they queued for plastic pints, huge portraits of great actors above them.

Cashback? asked the barman.

Twenty. No, fifty. Thanks.

They went into the pit. The crowd roared as the two lads came on stage and the opening riff beat the room into a living thing and the band matched them, songs you knew before you knew them, hair sweat and leather and they got back arms outstretched and reaching. In the one slow song, the wise hurt of their best lines stung Darragh out, like some weird hex, so true his toes curled in his Cortez. Give me younger us.

She was just across the river, seven minutes away, eight now, nine as she stepped into The Black Sheep. She explained it all to Aaron, the ticket mix-up, that it was completely over with Darragh but she was trying to be sound, her fear of the potential for mountainous weirdness and she was flustered and babbling by the time she saw he was amused and it was grand. He just thought it was gas.

We'll see them again, he said and he ripped the tickets clean in two. She gasped. He let the pieces fall and a few heads looked over like it was a proposal, and she collected the pieces from the floor. He brought his face to hers and kissed her. She kissed him back, their lips over each other, and her eyes closed, she pictured the two of them at future festivals.

When the lights came up Darragh cast around for her but he never caught her across the room. Buoyed by booze and sweaty solidarity they stayed out after and the shouted songs stayed in their ears. It seemed like everyone was out and with it the chance to still run into anyone. He got the strong ones when it was his round. His mam told him at the funeral that his uncle had a trick. People thought he was generous, she'd said, never stingy, but it was only so he could get a short in while he was up at the bar.

Back out amongst the kegs, Gav blew a tunnel of papal smoke into the night. Darragh stared straight ahead in the dripping alley until Gav spoke again.

Got fired today.

Fuck off.

Gav pulled out his phone to prove it and read out the formalities with relish, beautifully distanced from it all.

You were late, after two previous verbal warnings and one formal warning. When asked to give a reason for this, your given reason was that the World Cup was on. When asked to clarify this, you said that England got knocked out. While this was honest, it was not acceptable. Then she says, have you anything to say for yourself Gavin?

Did you?

Yeah. Think I was still locked.

What did you have to say for yourself?

Told her Wu Tang is for the children.

Darragh laughed and took the spliff off him.

I've a load of shit to give her back, Darragh said.

Gav shook his head like he was trying to shake something out of it.

No. Back of the wardrobe. Back in with everything you'll never throw out.

There should be an amnesty, Darragh said. For all the evidences of your exes.

Yeah, once a year, Gav said and Darragh pictured all the single earrings, the souvenirs and snags and all your faded favourites that you can't ask for back.

Give all their shit back to them.

Some hope, Darragh said. Maybe bonfire the lot.

Yeah.

Stack up the palettes and let it burn off.

Leave that to the loyalists.

But it's loyalty isn't it? Fucking . . . loyalty to someone's sock.

They slurred their way through town. He got to himself late, snakes in his mind, wondering about the times they'd argued. He said nothing to his mate until they both should have been home.

Hannah watched the fabric shift between Aaron's shoulder blades as he waited at the bar and she wondered if he could cook and when he came back she asked him.

Yeah, I'm alright. Like I'm past oven pizzas, he said.

Fair play.

Thanks.

My flatmate got that Salt Fat Acid book, she said.

Don't trust celebrity chefs, he said. Fucking . . . smug dealers.

I know but she's grand. Only cookbook ever had us using more salt.

The Samin of knowledge, she said, and saw he had no idea what she was talking about.

That's her name, she said.

The Samin of knowledge?

Doesn't matter. Every time I'm home I stress about how much my dad's using.

She must have thrown too much concern onto her face when she said it.

Salt, she explained. How much salt he's using.

He relaxed then. They fell quiet and she worried it would spread.

Isn't pepper doing well for itself? he said out of nowhere.

Pepper?

Pepper. Going around with salt. Not pulling its weight is it?

She snorted, a weird hoggy noise, not a date sound. It had always embarrassed her, and she threw a hand to her face but he didn't laugh and she was grateful for it. She could feel herself charging in.

Getting away with murder, pepper, she said.

Nah, think that's salt.

They never checked their phones. They never thought to. She watched him when he reached for his pint. Their glasses were the same level and he didn't keep an eye on hers like Darragh used to, or cock his head back every time: Aaron didn't need the expando gulp. Small tells, or small mercies. Darragh's eye bags and teeth had started showing all his nights. She had been about to put up with all of him and now she wouldn't have to, wouldn't have to watch him sink them too fast and keep her out too late. The flutter and climb of their conversation and she knew she was reading too much into everything, but she liked this frisky agony.

Come to mine? she asked him.

She got a flash of panic when she saw his surprise.

Now? he asked.

Not now . . .

Now's good.

OK.

They left just after and their laughs rattled from the backseat of the taxi as it spun them home. It was the first night they'd gone back to hers. Everyone was asleep and she led the way up the stairs, and in her room it was the perfect rush, standing as they yanked the tops off each other and she brought him down and it was hungry and tough between them. They both came and collapsed into each other and they wore the same smile in the dark. She was slushy with emotion but even near to sleep she couldn't stop herself speaking.

Best napkin ever.

His reply wasn't really words but his drowsy murmur made her feel safe. I've a good few blank spots, she wanted to say, and you fill me in. But she just snuggled in deeper and listened to his breathing slowing. Hold your hope fast, wear all the right shit, play the right games, dodge the wrong ones, check in enough but not too much, be sound understanding ballsy and above all hot and then sit back and wait for him to go distant but nothing was wrong yet, all new gags, all diamond wink and glitter, no flaws yet and they slept sweat slick and clutching each other and their date lasted the weekend.

o

Darragh had to work the weekend then found himself with his week free from Wednesday. It was a day to be out in the giving air, a day to go swimming, or at least talk about it and end up in a beer garden. He texted Gav.

- What you at?
- Pint to self.
- Where?
- Only having the one.

Darragh typed fast.

- Go on.
- Not today Satan.
- Tomorrow Satan?
- Yeah. Give you a shout.

He went to a pub where no one from work would be. He'd hidden her earphones in a drawer in his room, so he had no tunes and no choice but to listen to the nearby lads who were busy loosening ties and shouting in acronyms, who kept saying, not on my watch. He changed location and went on a solo run up on the high stool beside some aul lads, a horse school of burgundy shróns. He was sure it showed in public, a neon totem above his head, flashing arrows pointing at him like some gaudy motel.

He walked home in the fuzz and grain of closing dusk. Everything felt like last chance balloons. Stakes is high. The rules had changed but no one explained how, go work it out on your own and see if you could learn anything next time round. The chess of it and seeing now it was only checkers before. When to go staking claims and when to leave them alone. Maybe you left them alone too long then they were gone. There were weeks he didn't see her in front of him in the dark of the cinema or see her vanish round corners in town at night. There were weeks that didn't happen. The rest was not mapped.

At Christ Church the salty waft found him and yanked him back to an early time of theirs in the heady first weeks, the night waiting for the two of them, when they'd left the pub bound for comfort, wrapped up thick together against the cold, licking crispy bits in the dark.

He'd no idea what year it was or what was going on with the stampede outside the window and Darragh woke hurting. It was late October now. He realized it was the marathon pounding by outside. Some people lost things. He was one of them. It was always a country accent asking him the same questions and he feared they could see how many times he'd woken up without his bank card. Was it the same lad staring at a screen in a call centre every Saturday afternoon, the same lad who wasn't out last night? Was there an office pool in an industrial estate on when he would ring in again? He used googlemaps to work out how long he was conked out in Roma II, how much kip he'd managed slumped against shining Formica, as punters clattered, shoulder-sliding along the tiles, clutching trays of garlic cheese chips. He'd lost phones that way too and never got a proper answer off the lads behind the counter. They must have seen something while he slept. His sheets had sprung free at the corners – even they were trying to get away from him. The flat was just lads and no women, a leaning tower of bog roll tubes climbing the wall beside the jacks.

Terror jumped him at the laptop's low-battery warning. That was new. He kept getting hauled back to the summer, when they ran into each other, the night of the final, a couple weeks after the gig. That night remained tiny fishbones stuck and snared in his throat. He had reckoned he had got Delaney's in the break-up. Out the back the sun caught the fluttering little flags of all the countries above them. Gav had money on the Croatians. Darragh stuck a bet on with Gav's app and the back yard filled as they drank and hoped.

Modrić you goblin, Gav muttered.

Track your lives to footballers and whatever that was, it wasn't helping.

Same again?

Yeah, go on.

Darragh stood, levering himself off the table. The hatch was blocked by lads on stools so he went in and then he saw her, alone, waiting to be served. He slowed into stumbly steps, and she turned and saw him as he came over. She spoke first.

Hey.

Story?

He went in for the hug, knowing she'd smell it reeking off him. They stepped back and looked at each other. He thought she looked scatty. But then she wasn't half-cut.

You well? he asked.

Grand, yeah, she said, no complaints.

Sure who'd listen?

This is it.

She tried to keep her eyes on Darragh but she knew she was on borrowed time, knew what was coming. This should be grand, she told herself. We're all adults. Or we all should be.

Who you here with? she asked him, maybe a little fast.

Just Gav, Darragh said.

She thought this was nearly like first dates again: keep asking them questions. She was sorry that she had suggested coming here. Thick, obvious, asking for it.

Here, he said, let me buy you a pint.

She shook her head quickly.

Nah you're grand.

It's only a pint, he said.

You don't have to.

I know I don't have to. I'd like to.

Then Hannah saw Aaron, emerging from the jacks, over Darragh's shoulder. She looked back to Darragh as Aaron grew closer and then he was here and the three of them standing close.

Darragh, she said, this is Aaron.

Then Darragh understood and looked at him – comparison club, couldn't help it can't stop already playing it and Aaron was a handsome lad – then back to Hannah, everyone frozen in awkward.

How ya doin' Darragh. Aaron.

What's the story Aaron? What you having? I'm getting her one.

Nah man, you're grand, Aaron waved him away.

We're only having the one, Hannah said.

Darragh was too forceful now.

No, he said. I'm buying both of you a pint.

Aaron looked to Hannah for guidance.

OK, she feebled out.

Darragh turned to get served but the barman was right down the other end. He felt his face flushing and their eyes go between each other and return to him.

Four please.

Thanks, Darragh.

The wait for Guinness was extending the torture. Darragh shifted some beer mats around in the dead time. Hannah wanted to be anywhere else than here. For all of them.

Darragh aligned the beer mats and Aaron checked his phone. Eventually the barman set down the pints and Darragh paid for them and moved each a couple of inches towards its owner.

There you are, Darragh said.

Thanks.

Yeah, cheers Darragh, Aaron said.

No bother, Darragh said. Good to see you, he told Hannah.

Yeah, you too, she said.

Take it easy, he said. Nice to meet you, Aaron.

You too.

She raised half a hand to Darragh as he made to leave.

I'll let you go, Darragh said.

See ya, they both said.

He took his two pints back to the table where Gav had seen everything.

Y'alright?

Never better.

They kept at it until a teenager with lightning at his feet finished it, Mbappé drilling it home from outside the box.

It was a goth tester of a summer's day. Hannah woke early and cycled over to Kate's, breezing through the fresh blue morning. They drank diesel-strong coffee while the sun buttered up Kate's kitchen. They walked the South Wall, one of those fabled five days a year that truly held heat. Hannah's mood matched Kate's and they laughed easy. Kate had drawn a line under the weekend before, sworn off the sauce for her wedding in June. A boy flew his drone above the dog-walkers that sprinkled the beach. Suddenly at the start of the sea wall Kate hopped up onto a boulder and growled in her best Busta Rhymes, Gonna be another one of them hot summers.

Hannah smiled at this anthem of their youth and leapt up onto a rock opposite, like when they took to table tops together at festivals and didn't come down til dawn, and Kate slalomed through the verse, knocking through every intricate syllable and Hannah was laughing so hard she was barely ready to sing her part and as they sang, Hannah wondered what songs Aaron knew off by heart. There was so much she didn't know yet. Kate talked of first songs up and past the swimmers' club. Hannah kept quiet as they walked over the haphazard stones stretching out into the sea. There were no songs for this, this slow game she had to play. There were no songs for not leaping, not rushing and not tumbling. There were no songs for how much caution was needed. They got 99s and licked raspberry syrup from their sticky fingers. She gazed out the window as Kate drove them back. Across the strand clouds smuggled the pallid sun. She wouldn't tell Kate about Aaron, not yet, her plans a hall of shining lights. With someone new, you rat yourself out sooner or later, so full of their affection you can't keep it to yourself. She would wait. The sky spilled silver onto the dirty honey sand and she was exhausted by the hope of him.

THE SLUAGH

The night before she dreamt they came for her, and in the space before sleep she sensed them and they knew her too, her sadness like whale song they knew as their own, a call to hearts caved in, then spawning and turning in the pitch, the dangers of secrets and tongues, shadows dancing and forms shifting, sending shrieks sawing from below the nesting cliffs before rearing louder and rising like locusts, seeding dreams arachnid in the heads of sleeping children and she ran, from memories birthed and broken from the street and the end went unremembered but when she woke in half-light they flew from the spectred sides of her vision, before she dipped back and down and drifted deeper and deeper until silence swallowed it all.

Another night in Scooptown. The wipers of the taxi were no match for the angry rain, and the gutters filled and spluttered like an aul lad hacking up. Nina couldn't afford to keep hopping into cabs like this but if she got out now she'd be soaked to the bone.

Sometimes when I can't sleep, I watch them sleep, he said. The taxi driver found her eyes in the rearview and she looked away.

The Nigerians, he said.

He'd told her she looked tired when she got in. Minutes later he confided he wasn't sleeping himself, and now this. She'd only been awake a few hours, heartened by the dark when it came. Last thing she remembered before crawling upstairs was staring out into their tiny backyard, adding fag ends to the flowerpot as dawn turned lavender past the washing line.

You know the Circle K by the port? After a shift, I do watch them having their naps.

The taxi driver, seemingly encouraged, eyed her again and he laughed.

Now maybe I'm mad but if I knew I was, I wouldn't be mad, would I? he said.

Town was a purpling bruise she kept pressing. Town felt full of places she couldn't go now, the old pubs marked, whole streets cursed. They rolled past slurs of orange light outside, the downpour relentless. Things were getting a little harder and a little faster. She was thinking that she'd been out of her depth a few months. To stop any more intrusions from the front she made a show of taking her phone out and texted Badger.

- How'd the viewing go?

He read it immediately and he sent a stark black and white picture and her breath went back into her: a factory floor and a line of stripped bodies on their knees, stapled into each other mouth to anus.

- This was me earlier, third from the back.

- Badger.

- Human Centipede 2, if you're into it.

- I'm not.

Badger had been her best lad mate, maybe her best mate full stop, since they shared a gaff in Kilmainham in the lost years and she'd come to rely on him more recently. Say that for Badger, he was reliable, least early doors. If it was all transactional, why would mates be any different, plus it suited Badger too: behold my friend who is also a human woman. They could go hiding in public together while he looked around for someone to lead along for a couple months and then without fail hit eject before it fused into anything as stressful as a relationship. She saw them coming and she saw them go. Some of her wished she fancied him all the same. More of her wished she fancied girls. Gutter water sliced and spumed as they sped by the giant pillars of the Mary Immaculate and she was back, sparing thoughts, caught in visions of her granny making her tiny pilgrimages, lighting candles for half the street. In the end she was carried off by an enlarged heart and Nina got stung by that too, a heart too big for this world, too much and not able. The driver slowed, a red light where the road split.

I hit someone here.

He slipped the words out, discreet as a mother giving her wayward son money in public. The words filled the confines of the taxi. She felt the air thicken.

Cyclist. Course it was a cyclist. Young one came out of nowhere. Hopeless.

The silence crept and grew. She looked out the window and wished she lived in another city, one not pockmarked with her own life. She got out and she didn't tip him and he called her love. Still nothing back from Carla, still waiting, waiting for when Carla would wait for her. Might be waiting. They were supposed to go to college together but she didn't get into NCAD and Carla did. Nina got IADT instead and in fairness it wasn't anything like school. She'd waited for Carla enough times around Thomas Street, one time watched a raging student fly out from under the arch and stuff an entire portfolio into a bin a man was trying to light. Nina was only half the drama of some of them but then she always fell hard, like when she couldn't sleep on school nights unless she listened to CrazySexyCool start to finish. Proper drama, burning your fella's house down. But Left Eye was the one dead. Two years after, working in a gallery thinking that anyone who likes writing artists' statements shouldn't make art, she'd got the fuck out of Dublin before the brightest brats got their own exhibitions and she'd be asked to hand out the free wine. Two years back now and she thought she must look like the sculptures from college, half wronged woman half mantis, a Germaine Richier surrounded by contours and fillers that made girls younger than her look like shocked rubber ducks. She used to love town in the mornings, back when nobody had a job. Loved it just after nine, with the whole day ahead, like school when the bell goes and the corridors turn silent, empty and open. Now it just made her feel ancient. Before she left Dublin the best nights were over anyway. It ends just as it begins, everyone checked out everyone else as she pushed through the crowd. Carla had left her with no choice tonight, and once she was too busy when it counted Nina had got straight on to Badger and now she found him down the back, swaying by the smokers.

Am I late? she asked him when she landed at the table full of lads.

Tell you who's fucking late, he said.

She wished she'd known Badger's lad wasn't here yet. She could still be in bed. Badger stayed in communion with his phone. She found herself stood across from one of his mates, a shaggy lad in a garish zip-up. She only knew him from being out – his name gone or never there and too late to ask now. Badger told them he'd be back soon and melted off into the crowd. She got a pint and supped it with his mates, pure ratbag solidarity. They were all waiting. They all wanted the same things. Every ad was about Brave but she didn't see herself in that cute girl. Brave felt the weather against her. Brave had her business account closed on her without warning due to inactivity and she found out tax week. Brave got a real job now and took six months to get one print right. Something to do in the evenings. Brave still felt far from mortgages, winter breaks and Educate Togethers.

Bring out your dead, Badger's mate said to himself, as he wrestled and flopped down his pouch onto the busy table and started to extract scraggly clumps of tobacco hair.

Was watching this doc, right, so all the boys in World War 2, in the one-man submarines, all out of their minds, they were.

The lad's eyes drifted down to her chest as he talked. Getting angry at lads is throwing good energy after bad. Lads clamping eyes on the moving target of waitress ass. Lads pulling shit like getting into nothing scraps, pigheaded wars cooked up by drink. Lads with the death grip, lads letting themselves off the hook, lads going out to a match and winding up in the canal, or an ambulance. Lads lads lads.

Want some? Badger's mate asked, offering Nina the burning roach nub.

She took one sharp hit and gave it back.

That's the difference between booze and smoke, man, he said. Booze makes you quiet on the inside and loud on the outside. Smoke makes you loud on the inside and quiet on the outside.

She chose his right eye to concentrate on while he giddily yapped and yapped. His mate came on and it was mostly what she expected. House promised better but techno only promised more. More and more she only wanted full-on fuck-off panel beaters. Nina watched Badger's mate build his set. It was a full pint later when Badger returned.

Bit soft for you is it? he asked.

Shut up. Get sorted?

Badger nodded and eyed the crowd.

Ain't too proud to beg, she said and he dug in his pocket and fished out the bag and palmed it over. She'd never understand baggie design. It never sold or stopped anyone on the contents. Intricate weed leaf, Acid House smiley face, Chinese dragon, Playboy bunny. She licked and dipped her pinky into the little crystals and he smiled when she winced at the nasty chemical tang. She grimaced and drank.

Fucking gulf, he said.

Hah?

Gulf between how it tastes and how it makes you feel, he said, already brightening and Nina swallowed big mouthfuls of her sudsy pint. Things only held hope in the dark, when she couldn't see three feet in front of her, before all the afters, before the getting home, before work, before Suicide Tuesdays. The rain kept going like the streets deserved it and they were pinned under the shelter as things dropped off. She kept rubbing the back of her neck. Animals rising. Only now it was grand that she would never have her own show, that all those things were put away, that the only time she made anything at all was when she was dancing.

She felt the surge and it was a hot buzz and burn and they went in. She was laughing and she found herself nodding harder. On the decks Badger's mate was pushing it now. Live for nights, blasted clear, when the bass kicks the room back together. The pneumatics drove them on, hard and dogged, drum machines pounding in them, lifting them altarfacing and weightless, no doubt or halting fear, arching towards radiance and open to blinding yes.

o

Clouds darkened and shaped themselves and they rose and cir-
cled above, shunned by their old skins and spat to the skies this
shrouded mass, earthspurned and cursed together, condemned to
beat on, down the face of the rented earth and they were versed in
shadows, this mangled flock. The wind tore at them and they moved
cloaked and it had been dark for hours now and the horde grew
closer, leaving innocents below, screeching and sucking in whis-
pers, an hour where anything was possible and the world seemed
new to them, theirs an orb-eyed procession with skin pale as spi-
der's silk, bound together in restless pact and left to careen through
the wreckage and again they took to the hunt, rasping for their
prey.

The lights snapped on, cracked plastic cups swept up and
they were all moved on. The heads that can't go home, dazed,
blinking and sweating, session penguins huddled together
for warmth and promise. She shivered as Badger chased
options. If home was thinking about Rob, that was no choice
at all. Nervy smokes sucked down and she thought she heard
her lungs whistle.

Carla not out, no? Badger asked.
Badger fancied Carla and Nina didn't have the heart to tell
him he was on a hiding to nothing.

She could be yet, Nina said. Who's to say with her? Sometimes I'm not sure she exists.
She held her phone close to her nose ring until it swam into
focus.

Last seen yesterday at eleven eighteen, buddy.
Badger nodded, his jaw going ninety. The rain was firing back
off the pavement when it hit and a few seconds left them
soaked. She locked her phone. It always sounded like an
insect to her, mandibles clacking and closing, just as Badger

made a squawk of delight and told whoever was on the phone he'd see them soon.

C'mon you, Badger said to her. Night's like a shark.

It has three rows of teeth?

It stops moving and it dies. Anyways, Paddy's getting evicted.

Who's Paddy?

Ah you know Paddy.

She gave him a blank look.

They're getting fucked out so he's having a wake for the gaff.

She got in the taxi with Badger and his mates, riding the neon blur and shake of it, past the packed chippers, the gangs, the broken glass and the escape rooms. It kept lashing, hammering everything, the cobbles slicked and smudged into underworlds of wet reflections. Run from the house but nostalgia is always the knife.

There were rumblings in the last of the Portobello gaffs and Nina watched the taxi slush away through pools of warm sodium and leave the red-bricked warren. She hoped Carla would show her face. They packed themselves tight to the door, a giddy knot grinning at the clangour beating within. She gripped her phone tight in her jacket pocket. She'd been testing herself. Give it another few. Some of them probably knew. The door flew open to reveal Paddy, a man in a dressing gown already feral with pleasure. Badger was right. She did know Paddy. He looked at them, bright and wired.

My friends! Please, be welcome in my home. You will enjoy. They piled in and she was introduced to Paddy again.

We've met, he said.

Yeah, think so. Sorry they're selling.

They're not fucking selling. Come on.

Paddy led them through, Badger granting hugs as he went, Nina in the rearguard. A mattress leaned against the wall beside a faded poster that read Stay Home. Everyone was smashed. She recognised half of them and knew no one. They'd been here as a pair before. She remembered Rob on the couch she now passed, in that faded t-shirt like he was born into it. Seemed like he'd never charged a phone in his life and it was off more than it was on and she'd loved that at first. Everyone talked about getting off the grid; Rob actually did it. But when it's your fella the novelty wears off. It wasn't some great act of sabotage against our addiction to screens. He was just shit with phones. But she wasn't going to think about him. She wasn't going to think about much as she trailed Badger to the hectic kitchen.

How was last night? Badger asked Paddy as their host hauled fresh cans out the bottom of the fridge and passed them round.

Mental, Paddy said. Fucking palace of mental.

Deadly.

Nina and Badger watched two girls, legs intertwined, going ninety on a bag between them. In turn their heads flew back from a key.

Hungry Hungry Hippos, Badger said.

That'll be good for conversation, she said.

My little brother calls it bird seed, she said.

She did a hectic woodpecker impression for him, imitating the crazed stabbing of beak.

Peck. Peck peck peck.

He laughed, then stopped, checked himself.

Hang on, you've a brother?

Yeah, she said. Younger brother.

No you don't.

No, pretty sure I do yeah.

Badger looked up to the low stained ceiling as he turned the information over in his racing skull.

Never knew that, he said.

Yes you did.

He considered it again, then shrugged. She wasn't mad, not at Badger anyway. Blame doesn't work in percentages, she'd learned that. Rob said he never knew when he turned into a sessioner. But one day you're having a smoke and the next you're a smoker. You're a smoker when you know somewhere on you is a lighter. It went late around her. There was enough room to dance with the coffee table pushed back and she joined a couple moving because they had to and she had enough vortex in her to be with them. She was glistening and running her hand through her hair by the time she sat back down. From across the mess Badger, moving towards her with his hand guiding a girl's back, shouted over. Nina shouted back and when he got closer, she felt the girl's half eyes on her. He squatted down in front of her with the zealous popping eyeballs of a fanatic. She grinned at him.

Here, I'm heading off, he said.

Who's your mate?

That's eh, that's my cousin.

Is she, yeah?

He looked delighted with his own lie, throwing Nina rabid little nods of his head.

Yeah, we're gonna do some bonding.

Keeping it in the family?

Yeah. Give you a shout.

She let them go then. Are we all selfish fucks, she wondered. These are selfish acts. We're only able to keep going because we're all selfish. She was glued to the cracked brown couch. It reminded her of those dogs with all the folds in their faces. She'd read they got rotten problems from all the surplus skin: airless trenches crammed with festering bacteria. She smoked until a lad appeared beside her, methodically lowering himself backwards over the couch until his spine was where his arse should be. His legs hinged over the back as he chatted at her, his face at lap level.

Blood not go to your head down there? she asked him.

You can make an accommodation with it.

Now the lad's mate sat down beside them, his jaw tight, his breath beery.

How's tricks? I'm with Monkeyboy here.

Yep, this is my fellow session clown.

Any joy with those cans we stashed bro?

Long gone. Shoulda stuck them in the hedge.

As he talked, she nodded for him but she was somewhere else, seeing flashes of Rob and the nights he went away, distant after smoking himself still and how many nights that was. The first time she ever saw him she'd felt stripped by her need for him, a hot hard pain. She wanted him to love her, she wouldn't take like for a second, her guts in a seizure off him and he must have seen it too. What had she told him before she ever opened her mouth.

The bass landed hard and a couple screamed. Empty cans wobbled as a lad knocked into the table and made a big show of apologizing. She tried not to check her phone, failed. Last bank holiday she'd found Rob and his mates playing snipers on a rooftop at dawn, out of their minds, crouched and hiding from each other. She watched him up there, them and him, him of them, and remembered again how his face glowed peach in the sunrise. She used to text him wb. Fuck it. It's always write back. Your heart is undermining your best laid plans every chance it gets. She came back to the room. She smiled at the heads closest to her. She had their attention and the rest was easy.

Want to stick your beak in?

Nice one.

She snapped her head straight back after the snort. Something nice in the recoil. The joy buzzed up too hard inside her. The room was nodding with her and she lit another smoke. She spied a spare can wedged under the couch. She rescued it, cracked it and horsed down fizzy swallows. A young one in angel wings corkscrewed through the bodies. No sign of Carla. Carla, who could jump into any sesh but jump out too. Carla, who lost boys and clothes other people would never have in the first place and didn't blink. Carla would shut down the lads beside her, these two telling Simpsons jokes to each other and rocking hard in laughter. The session roared around her but she stayed sunk where she was. Hard false delight surging through her. Felt grand. Across the sticky table someone was speaking to her. She dragged her vision up past ashtrays, spilled matches, skins soaked and accordioned, a Coke bottle glugged out and empty. A lad was staring at her. His frame was humming.

D'you want to do the honours? he asked and flicked a finger towards a laptop balanced at a demented angle next to her. She swivelled and stared at the screen, all blinding glare and blank. She couldn't think of a single track. Blank. She was running out of time to choose the next one. The track kept counting down. She let someone else muscle in, let something else take over. Paddy swung his head in and glared at a couple of lovers lingering by the open front door, their fingers interlocked.

Fucksake lads! Batten down the hatches.

o

*A ragged hunting party with one pack heart between them, past keen-
ing, a conspiracy gladdened by its bad intentions, carriers of wounds
and lacerations and they found fault fast and tore at themselves too,
in their thin flesh a shared distrust for sunlight, boils of hurt under
dark eider, with the godlightning in their veins, pinions at full reach
above the city and they wheeled and they were in descent and too late
they packed malice, that was their lot, talons bared and their quarry
known, a twisting riot and venom in screeching celebration of what
was to come and they swung round terracotta corners and cawed and
clawed and they were within the canals now.*

She climbed the narrow stairs and let herself down in a
smaller room. The sneaky thrill when they first met, back
when Rob was with a mate of Carla's and now, looking back
– and she worried she did nothing else – she knew it was a
klaxon she wasn't up for hearing until it got out of hand. If
it happened to her it can happen to you. No. It happened to
her, then it happened to you. Breath that should have been
hers had been pushed into another girl's ear and sometimes
you had to face facts, or even just the one. Fact was, the Elf
had won. The Elf had him. She thought of the three of them
at Body & Soul and then she tried not to think of the bad
lurking back there. Just then a happy clamour announced
Carla's arrival. Carla, the Teflon sesh monster, Carla charmed
and careless. She hugged her way through the room and Nina
watched the flowers dance on the back of her jacket. It was
Carla who christened Rob's new thing the Elf, on account of
her thin pointed features, a gorgeous miniature who smiled
big and said little. For all they knew, Carla maintained, she
was hiding proper elf ears in that double-blonde hair. Nina
knew better: she'd seen those ears up close: helix piercings

but definitely, disappointingly, humanoid. Finally, Carla sank onto the bed beside her and hugged her, a good hug.

Heya, Carla said.

Nice to be granted an audience, Nina said, but anger was impossible.

Sorry. Passed you on the bus couple days ago.

You should have hopped off.

This was Thursday, Carla said. You were opposite Chop-Chop.

Yeah?

Yeah.

Carla's eyes flicked up to her. Nina would make her say it now.

Looked like you were crying, Carla said.

Sounds about right, Nina said finally and her breaking little smile made Carla hug her.

D'you want to talk about it?

You're alright, Nina said.

Are you?

Yeah. Never better.

Nina gulped from her can and let it ripple down.

Listen, they're coming here. Rob and your one. Elfo.

She's not my one. Neither's he.

Sorry, Carla said and for once Nina thought she actually looked sorry. Just a heads up.

Thanks.

They fell silent in the howling room. Their heads rested on the wall behind.

D'you remember the ringing in your ears? Carla asked her, when you were fifteen? After you'd come home. Used to love it. Staring at yourself in the mirror. Hearing it go through you.

We can't hear it anymore. It's nerve endings. They're gone. They lit more smokes. They nodded along.

It's been a long time since we lost that, Nina said.

Yeah.

Forgot to get nostalgic about it.

After racing seconds Carla kissed her on the head and stood.

Gotta run babe, Carla said.

What?

I only called in to say hi.

Stay. For a bit.

Sorry love. Promised myself I'd be good for once.

Carla left her alone with herself then. Rob did the dirt on her. Say it another way. Say it another five ways there was nothing else, the three of them switched around with each other, then he switched her and the Elf to just the Elf. She loved it when time went away, but it was only weeks since all their fumes mixed sweat flesh and after, nothing. In the end, after watching an insect crawl inside the crimson nylon of the tent, after his fingers sliding down a body that wasn't hers, beside hers, fucking the Elf, and after, all three staggered out of the tent sticky and half naked still wild and ragged in the grey dawn, the tents drooped and sagging from the rain and lads slumped against fencing, pissing. All that weekend while she was staring into him, he was pouring his energies elsewhere. Life was getting shifted up and down on shame escalators that's all it was, all of this and she was stuck on them now. He always said he was sex positive but in the end he was just Elf positive and now when she thought of bodies she saw the two of them and her under them and covered in him and she stayed under the covers for a month after, tombed. She looked around. Carla was gone. It heaved beneath. Some lad was collapsed and snug by her rib, dead to the world. She concentrated on what was in front of her, the thick slugs of powder on the mirror. She bent to them. Before she lifted her head, she knew it was too late, knew she'd got it wrong, knew it was ketamine. Everything froze then. Everything distant and dislocated, pain vanishing, gone, out of arm's reach where your need can't get at it, and she hauled back, back past old scars and hands on new lovers' backs and tumble back, into dance floors of cold stone, dance through it all if you can stand and if you can stand it. She climbed into some crystal infancy. A chasm was opening inside her. Downstairs was shouting.

Fuck it, it's too late, just let them in.

It's a raid bitches!

They came from the west then and Rob led them and it was chaos with the host below. She heard him from a great distance and then she heard the Elf's stinging laugh and footsteps but she was stuck. Then the door swung open and she saw the two of them, his arm slung over her, smiling.

Screams then it goes quiet and she misses that too and he is already too late as he nears her, like only he can see her and she can see the Elf too and she can only watch his fingers failing and it will always be too late, his hands on her again, a final insult before the ambulance and her blood failed her, as numbed scale grew and grew and gave her everything and she sees herself rising up, towering over all of them and she leaves the room behind and flying down the street never looking back her breath climbing frost in the fresh black air and she reaches the canal and she steps light onto the low wall and from there a new view and she stumbles, her foot finds air and she's all air until everything is dark ice and she sees all this but she can't move she can't speak her chest is not hers and her heart was stopping.

DOG MEN

Shake his hand
Check your fingers still there
Hope shit might be different this time

The dog track shines through the dark. He never blinks, gives
no inklings, and dog man don't talk. For now he smokes near
the pillars and no one pays him no nothing as they go by, dog
man as much part of the track as the steps and the hoard-
ings, and he has his usual thick trackies on and the fur of his
parka hood sits round his skull like some great thuggish car-
rion. He has huge hands, columns between the knuckles. He
reaches back and itches the satisfying slug of fat that marks
the end of his neck. He was a mammoth from birth, a big
unit raised by big units: dropping that babba be like dropping a Tonka trunk, they said. Before he worked for Maguire,
he was bouncing under his da in Q Bar, back when it was Q
Bar. But working with family was no use, bad enough without pissed students in shirts roaring at you that you'd still
be here in five years and they wouldn't. He has never made
a sudden movement in his life. Too much shite talk and too
many shite hawks, his da used to say. He got gone after that
and now dog man keeps his own counsel. He waits. He taps

his ash and watches it fall. He pulls on the smoke again and feels it inside him.

Shane and Jayden are nearly there after the long drive, but Shane will take them the long way round, through Ringsend so they don't go past the protests at the front gates. Shane wonders if this is only for his own sake; he is forever guessing what his son knows and what he doesn't. Shane knows what they say, the women outside with their placards and sandals, shouting at any punters heading in on foot, turning it into a walk of shame. Old dogs get retired to hot countries, Shane told him. Wouldn't mind that myself, he'd said after. They'd got Jayden an iPad for his eleventh birthday but he's not allowed bring it up to his room. Jayden said he's been left out but left out of what, Shane wanted to know.

The view of that classy nest of a stadium downriver lights his blood every time. He can't help it. Dee has him banned from talking about it at home, says it winds him up something rotten. But it should. You can't make it up with the FAI. Every time Shane took cash out of the ATM he thought of that clown of a CEO, pulling out three hundred quid at a time just for walking around money. Fifty grand for a James Bond cake while the grassroots rot. He takes Jayden to the Ireland matches all the same. He's defended himself over that and he will again if she has another go. Yes, he paid for the season ticket. Yes, it was a waste of money. No, he doesn't regret it. It can't be inevitable they're brutal. It's the hope that kills you. Long balls at the end of the world.

They take the early right off the South Lotts and Shane lifts two fingers off the wheel to let another van with the same idea go first. The van in front is a yellow reg, the English trainers rolling off the ferry and only up the road from the port. Trainers coming from all over the midlands and beyond, Kilkenny, Tipp, Kerrymen, syndicates and security. There are thirteen races on tonight and Shane doesn't like the number, a tempting of fate he distrusts as he guides the van between the narrow breeze-block walls and into the trainers' yard. But he's been excited since the draw last week. It was a draw you could have a go at.

He finds a spot and rumbles the Transporter to a stop. He cuts the engine and he and Jayden climb out. Their doors shut in solid harmony and Shane slides open the back, where Breakfast Roll tests the bars with his thin snout. The greyhound's torso is shaped like a wave and his rib cage expands as he breathes, the intricate bones rising out, hung over lungs like balloons. Evenly stippled rows of tiny black points from where his whiskers launch, under the hardwired scoop of his muzzle. Shane leads the heel of his hand along the dog's tight tan fur and the dog sniffs hungrily up along it, his eyes antic in his narrow antelope skull. The insides of his papery ears bear his tattooed ID numbers. Breakfast Roll is three years old and all limbs and twitchy energy, and he changes direction with every flick and sniff. Jayden is still young enough that Shane can remember when, like the dog, his eyes seemed too big for his head. They get the dog out of the cage and Jayden gets the leash on and Roll steps in his careful, spindly way onto the ground. He makes pincery explorations and his swagging tongue falls lopsided from his maw. Shane locks the van and looks at his son, who knows what's coming next.

Where's your jacket?

Jayden throws his eyes to the floor as Breakfast Roll pants.

D'you not want to wear it?

There is no answer off Jayden. He doesn't want to say anything that might incriminate himself.

What's wrong with it?

Nothing.

Shane knows what's wrong with it. Some things held, some remembered. Life was hard enough without the right brands, he'd said to Dee back in August. They'd gone back and forth over it, but Jayden had ended up with a jacket he was ashamed of.

No moaning if you're cold, Shane says.

No moaning.

Maybe he's a dick to push Jayden, who was still learning the makes he needs, but too quiet yet to demand them. He's been thinking his son might bruise easily, and two months into secondary school Shane was convinced it was already happening and Jayden was keeping it to himself. There's a cop on in that, Shane knows, and he holds an unspoken respect in this, in his son's resolution. Jayden is caught between things and Shane holds shards from that age himself. He reckons everyone does. He wouldn't wish it on his worst enemy.

Breakfast Roll's wet button of a nose quivers. Shane bends down, stretching towards his toes and feels the strain behind his knees. He had been on early this morning, behind the wheel by six. They were timed on every delivery, hounded by the tracker. Like everything, it was a numbers game. A numbers game and a closed shop.

Jayden strokes the long esker of the dog's back. Shane sees the admiration for the dogs growing in his son and he is proud of it. They walk across the car park with only vans in it and the grandstand sparkles opposite and above it and beyond only black. The sound of the track and the tannoy reaches them. Jayden brings his head up from the dog to his dad.

Why's he crap?

What? says Shane, to buy himself time.

Breakfast Roll. Why's he crap?

He's not crap, Shane says, he's just a slow starter.

He's a slow finisher too.

He's just been unlucky, that's half of it. Lady Luck.

Jayden brings his lips together in thought before he opens his mouth again.

How come she's a lady?

Loads of things are women, Shane says.

Like what?

Boats.

Boats are women?

Yeah. Mother Earth. Woman.

Shane lets his son mull on this. Breakfast Roll picks his way along in his cautious spiny way.

Da.

Yeah.

Are we gonna lose again?

Shane stops in his tracks so Jayden does too. Shane makes a show of patting down his pockets.

What's up? Jayden asks.

It's only I left my crystal ball in my other jacket. Now shut up, you're wrecking his mojo.

What's a mojo?

Together they make for the weigh room, the dog between them.

The track is an unreal green, like the saturation is up too high. The tricolour flaps by the spiky palms. On the terrace Frank removes the thick frames from his plum nose and haws on them and his breath blooms in the night air and steams the glass like a pond frosting. He couldn't leave the house without them. It's worst when he's lost them in the morning, after he's gone to bed without them and stumbling around the empty kitchen, trying to steer and steady himself. The cruelty in not having the one thing he needs to find them. She used to say he was like a mole without them. He's been without her six years now. Most days he feels a drifting, and he finds himself walking for hours at a time. He likes the coast, and it amuses him how much better the beaches on the Northside are. He often walks Donabate, shelled and not part of things. He knows there are wallabies across the water on Lambay Island, little furry relics of an American dynasty with a penchant for exotic animals. Frank likes to think of them hopping about over there. It's one of those bits of trivia he loves: the Pheno in Dublin 8, the two O'Connell Bridges. He sits the frames back on his face and the world greets him sharp again. Half the hoarding was missing these days, BoyleSports and the odd one for Gain Feeds, but the rest of the brackets still up, holding nothing. He looks away from the track and towards the tote. The punters around them recede and then Carol stands out. She's got a face for kindness, his favourite kind, all the ones that tore at him down the years had some of it, and now her frizzing curls block her eyes as she takes a bet off someone. He sees Tom arriving. He does not know who is older. He puts great stock in their friendship, a surprise and a comfort to him, like a fiver found in a winter coat just as the weather snapped. Tom sets up camp beside him as the floating reserves are called over the tannoy.

Trap One plus one, says the commentator.

Frank and Tom mark down the changes in weight. Afterwards, Frank watches her for a few stolen seconds.

o

Above the terrace, in the bright stretch of the Grandstand Restaurant, Maguire holds the door open for Hazel and they greet the two girls behind the desk. Their date is thirty minutes young.

Great to see you, says one of the girls.

Time I showed my face, he says.

Hazel is between the ages of the girls and Maguire himself. He is known in here and Hazel knows it straight off but she plays along. They are shown to his usual table by the window. There's tells everywhere. It was full of little tests for her too, Maguire knew. The track wasn't for everyone. Different game since Harold's Cross shut and RTÉ did a hatchet job on their sport. No tv show anymore, half the crowds gone, but still Maguire keeps count. He counts everything. He has a head for numbers and it's paid off. He gets fitted by Louis Copeland himself when he needs a new suit and he'd beeped learner drivers on his way into town. He's running three bets tonight, nothing fancy. He has no time for the flashy young lads, twenty if they're a day, rolling up loud in new Range Rovers, but hopping out of them in tracksuits. He fixes his cuff and orders two Morettis to get them going. They will move onto red later. The paper placemat on the table invites Hazel to adopt a dog and Maguire watches as she reads it. Well over a thousand dogs got re-homed last year, it says, helping dogs find their forever home. He checks the races ahead. There's born railers and Sauna Winks was not one of them so they were giving him a hand in race four. Midweek was best. The student taking the bets arrives at the table, the one with the black nail polish, and Maguire thinks, not for the first time, that her manager should have a word about the nails.

Any bets? she asks.

Maguire looks to Hazel: she won't know to bring cash and she turns flustered when she is told as much by the student. She wants to pay her way and now she can't. He gets a satisfaction out of having guessed this right and he waves her away, opening his wallet to a crisp rack of twenties. He snaps out a few for her.

That'll get you started, he says.

Thanks.

He doesn't know her age, doesn't look them up beforehand. He hates online, full of moaners and feelings he has no time for. Online was for students and he was never a student, he'd gone straight to work. If he was the last generation that was true of, he was fine with it. He'd guess she's thirty-six. He'd guess separated. He knows she works in payroll. He knows he's just done that thing with his mouth that he tells himself not to do, makes him look too sharky. He checks the menu. He's no interest in what the soup is and never orders chicken for his main. The waitress, a young one he knows, arrives smiling to their table. He likes the waistcoats they wear, smart.

Hey yis. What can I get ya?

He shifts his glance to Hazel across from him.

You order for me, he says.

He enjoys this, seeing how she deals with being put on the spot, going over the options. She takes her time.

He'll have the steak, she says. And so will I.

How would you like them cooked?

Quickly I'm starving, he says.

Everyone has a laugh but the question hangs as it fades.

Medium for him, says Hazel, correctly.

His smile heads for the margins of his face and he nods at her, back to you.

And for yourself?

The same, please.

He winks at Hazel and the waitress tells them that's lovely and leaves. Her hands out in front of her on the white linen. He doesn't like when they check their phones too much. Her eyes flick to the track outside the glass, shining reflections and the hiving outside, then back to him. Their beers arrive and they clink a cheers and drink up.

My da first took me here, he says.

Oh yeah?

Yeah. Ah he loved it. He was a great man. He used to say he only ever had the one argument with my mam. Only it lasted thirty-seven years.

He crows on the punchline and Hazel gives him back a smile, half a laugh and he looks out to the track, his hand following the line of his lower lip, as he scans what happens out there, outside the glass.

Trainers and dogs mill around the windowless weigh room and dog man runs his eye over them all. Some he knows, the lifers. He was young for a lifer himself, but it is what it is. He sees Salvo Dunne coming in the door with a dog and they exchange nods across the room. He knows Salvo works for Maguire, knows Winks isn't Maguire's only dog and Salvo isn't his only trainer. Salvo used to offer to mark his card for him, but dog man has no card. He doesn't bet. It disagrees with him. His outer rock face does not change but he smiles inside: Salvo actually looks like a henchman, between the jacket and the hair pulled back. They both sorted people. Something fell off the back of a lorry, Salvo might be near it. Salvo had hooked him up with a dodgy box with all the channels last year. He might see him later. He hopes he won't.

How's the form, Salvo says, not expecting the response that he doesn't get.

Blue, they called the colour of dogs like that, a streamlined river of midnight muscle. Sauna Winks looks up at dog man and gets a good scratch behind the ears.

Sauna Winks. Trained him since he was a pup.

That was money for you, they knew, being able to own dogs and barely see them, only when you fancied a night out under the lights. Well for some.

Haven't seen the young fella, have you?

The pendulum head of dog man swings no.

Little bollix, Salvo says. Pups, ha.

Salvo gets a nod back, pups. But he seems able for it, Salvo says, and they'd know either way soon enough. He keeps moving. Salvo was always on the go, covering ground and making things tick, Duracell bunny fella. Not for him. He stays down here. Sometimes the dogs are in his sleep and he sees them like they are here, on the scales, looking at him, and then he can't move. But here they look at their owners, not at him.

Coming into the weigh room, Jayden's nose twitches like a cartoon bunny. Shane waits for the hot stink of piss to pass, thin rivers running from apologetic dogs, shivery things with sorry in their eyes. Dee is always on about the smell of the van and four times a week she says it makes her gag. Just as well she's never smelled a weigh room, Shane thinks. It was the concentration of the stench in here, a mecca for dog piss and Jeyes Fluid. Trainers in anoraks mutter as they record the weight of each dog as it stands skittish and febrile on the scales in the middle of the room. Still mad to Shane that the English dogs were kilos and Irish were in pounds. The world was so often the wrong way round. He looks down at his son.

He'd words with Dee about the purple shiner Jayden brought home two weeks back. He's a sensitive kid: too sensitive, Shane fears, and the knocks are coming. No harm, the right amount of knocks, but hard to get that right. Mammying him would hardly help, Shane'd said. They can't be worried about every lad in school. The lads waiting outside school were the ones to worry about. Shane had cousins like that, a new number every six months: piranhas in the tank. Shane and Jayden get Breakfast Roll up on the scales. The dog's expression suggests he knows he is being measured.

Perfect weight, Salvo says.

Yeah, spot on, Shane says.

Jayden pats and encourages Roll as he gets him down off the scales. For such speed merchants, they were gentle creatures, long, fine-boned bundles of nerves. Mannerly animals, and breakable-looking.

Trackside, Devin hustles past the old gents running the tote, the legends of the game under their monster umbrellas and one of them still in a long camel coat. The signs say sterling taken. Devin is fifteen and done with it. Devin knows how to get through the crowd, knows Henry Street on a Saturday, knows big families and small rooms and he is getting to know the track, a mad shop but he likes it. Young ones looking lethal, big men in full trackies, grumbling aul lads with scoured faces under flat caps, squeezing the form for dear life. Communion season, kids dressed up having their first flutter, flush with tenners, dickie bows and waistcoats. At the rail he stops and waits for Salvo. The dogs all in their traps, six by six by six, locked up in the kennels until it was go time. Salvo is grand, the soundest of any of them near the kennels. He got Devin out here twice a week, cash in hand and around animals. Salvo's never slagged him, never called him a short arse, even took him for a carvery once. Better than being on the block, probably what Salvo had promised Devin's granny before bringing him here the first few times. Devin's a fast learner. He remembers what he needs to, the things he hears around men. The dog is only as good as the diet. What dogs had track craft. He has seen the dogs carried off and no one had to lie to him. It's always the first bend. Dogs get injections sometimes. Dogs get fed sausages through the heats, fat and useless, and then no sausages and watch them tear the track up. Devin rocks on the huge bubbles of his VaporMax as dog man comes closer. He stares at the bulkhead of dog man's skull while in turn dog man looks at the lad's runners. Devin keeps his kicks clean, he'd told dog man that before, the lad makes them sparkle, half an hour with the Cif and the toothbrush. His own runners aren't bad yokes, but they look stale compared to the kid's. He looks at runners on his phone a lot, looks at the mental ones when he's bored. This might be the year the bubble might swallow the whole shoe. He even adds them to the basket sometimes, but dog man never puts in a delivery address or a card number. He catches himself, been admiring the lad's ones so much he's been tilting his head and he draws back up to his full six three.

Give us a smoke, Devin says to dog man.
Something funny about him, Devin thinks, this weird baldy giant in front of him, like talking to a rhino. A rhino'd talk more.

G'wan it's only cancer, Devin says, you might as well share it.
Dog man offers Devin the pack, and watches the punters. Devin snaps his Zippo shut and, exhaling, slings his elbows back and joins dog man regarding the dogs going by.

Ever think they look like aliens? Devin says.

Devin gets no reply, but feels they are both looking.

Alien lookin' cunts, Devin says.

Dog man regards the same dogs but offers no opinion.

Talk to ya.

He tosses the smoke, sparks cartwheeling in its wake. He keeps moving. He hasn't seen a derby yet. Salvo said that's where the real money is, the top bookies with their private security to whisk them out, could be a hundred grand in a suitcase. He knew where he was going with the cash he was making from tonight. He'd hit Brown Thomas last week with the boys. Savage craic, but they'd eyes on them from the minute they came in. They'd split up, winding up the Indian security fella who stalked them around the Canada Goose and the Hugo Boss and the Kenzo. He has his eye on a few things now and he's dying to get back in, this time with cash on him. He wants to lead the security lads around and then whip out his wallet and get himself whatever he wants. He's dying to see the look on their faces.

Jayden quickens his step, a little hop he's too young to contain, as he follows his dad through the crowd. His head bobbles about at different sights, not fixed on one man or thing. Shane sees Keith, looking as hounded as ever: his cousin has a face that looks like it's never seen a pillow.

Alright big man, Keith says to Jayden. You gonna win tonight?

Nah, says Jayden.

No?

Nah. He's not good enough.

No faith.

Keith looks conspiratorial to Shane.

Always someone else's fault with these kids, Keith says.
Shane pulls his head back, surprised at Keith.

Not him, now, Keith says quickly. Don't mean him.

Right.

The rest of them.

Jayden looks between the two men above him.

The young lad last week, has his mates over, Keith says.
D'you know what they call him? Fat Ronaldo, they call him.

About a legend, Shane says.

The fucking neck. You know the problem with them?
They haven't had their recession. Couple of the young ones
at work, same. Dozy bitches.

Keith stops himself. He knows he's overstepped it again and
he blinks. Shane watches him try to shake the instant bile
that just found him. Keith's eyes dart down to Jayden.

Want to get yourself a bar son?

Keith reaches for his pocket. Shane has his own hand in his
pocket fast to cut him off at the pass, and rummages up some
coins for his son.

Go on, Shane says, there's your vulture funds.

Jayden picks the two-euro coin from his dad's palm and heads
off, head up, chocolate on his mind and money in his paw.

You might place in this one? Keith asks.

We'll see, sure, Shane says.

This one . . . might not be for the likes of us.

Shane sucks his teeth at hearing this and Keith holds his
gaze and confirms it again for him with a fraction of a nod, a
strange set certainty in it.

Feel it in your waters?

Something like that, Keith says.

Keith walks off as Jayden appears from the throng, munch-
ing, watching the dogs get loaded in for the next race.

C'mon, Shane says. Let's stick something on him, yeah? They head over to the tote. He doesn't bet enough to have a favourite, but he heads over to the one run by a woman.

Sometimes, he tells Jayden, you've to put your money where your mouth is.

His hopes climbing and his son beside him, he writes his bet down. He goes for Breakfast Roll to win outright, not even each way. He hands over cash and gives the slip to Jayden, who clutches it tight and looks to the track.

Over on the terrace Frank is glued to the glossy pages of the race card and its big rectangles of primary red. He surveys the races ahead, sliding his thumb down. He checks the prefixes denoting the lineages of different dogs. It was all dynasties. Fifth race in and the dogs caper round the last bend, one with a clear lead.

Kiltimagh Dazzler takes the last curve well and first place with it, Naas Scrambler in two.

Leaning side by side against a barrier, Frank and Tom watch hard but it's the dust again for the dog they chose and as one they fuck their slips to the ground. The tannoy tells it.

The winning time at 28.56, Kiltimagh Dazzler.

Scuppered, Frank says.

They're favourites for a reason Frank.

You should have bet on him so.

Couldn't have you losing on your own. Moral support, says Tom, jowly and frowning beside him, as he scrutinizes the card and emits a low deep sound. Frank knows Tom has lost interest.

Tell you what I think, says Tom.

Treat me.

I think fuck this.

Might as well see it out, Frank says. Stay for one more.

Ah that was one more. Here.

Tom scribbles a name on a slip, and a rutted noise from the roof of his mouth tells Frank he's amused himself, and he folds it neatly and passes it to Frank.

I'll leave you with one, Tom says.

Safe home Tom.

It's not home I'm going to.

He cuffs Frank warmly on the shoulder as he leaves. Frank looks at the slip and opens it: it reads Norfolk Enchants. He says it aloud and too late it makes sense. He looks up, but Tom's back has already merged into the crowd. Frank looks for Carol. He sees Jackie first, dolled up and clacking her claws. Not making things easy on herself with the slips, he thinks, then his eyes find Carol. For years he's been coming here, seeing her twice a week and never knowing what to do when she held his look for more than a second. She looks up now and they lock eyes and are startled together by the act, before she brings her look away, and back to the hands and the slips and the notes before her. He keeps his head and hopes in the card again and sticks a little red bookie pen in his mouth and chews on it. He reads that Charity Maggie is a Special Lady, that Sauna Winks is one to watch, that Breakfast Roll needs to be at his very best, that Kylemore Wonder could put a marker down. Frank holds the pen above the slip, and it wavers, hovers there, then something takes him, the pluck of chance and the decision made, and he picks Breakfast Roll at 6–1.

At the rail Shane sips from a cup of tea. Jayden, swamped by Shane's jacket, is too young for hot drinks past a hot chocolate and there's no hot chocolate at the track. Under floodlights the track lies empty, luminous and exact between races, save for the blue tractor that slowly rakes the sand as it makes its rounds. Shane always thought they were lucky to have Jayden, after everything. The longest birth, the midwife told them, that she'd ever seen. Thirty-eight hours, like being trapped in a submarine as things went wrong. Seemed to Shane that with all the fights, all the smart nasty lines between himself and Dee, they had sullied their one son. He was realising there was more he couldn't fix than he could. It all went back to those chats with Dee about whether they'd go for another kid. That had been rough. A son, after years of trying, one was enough, one was winning the lotto, but she felt different and now it stained this gorgeous kid shivering beside him. Even when they weren't talking about it, they were talking about it. He remembered when the PlayStation 2 came out and suddenly you'd to call what you had PlayStation 1. It was only ever PlayStation. Shane and Jayden and Breakfast Roll join the parade, six handlers and their dogs.

Frank walks towards the umbrella showing the odds and the two women underneath. Carol looks up and smiles at Frank and another step forward and he is within smell and reach of her. He puts his hand out, offering her the slip.

Close last one, Frank, Carol says.

Not close enough, he says.

Jackie scrunches her face up.

Carol I need a coffee, Jackie says, I'm dying on my feet here.

Carol nods assent and Jackie's off, talking as she grabs her bag.

It's my own fault, explains Jackie. Drank myself into Bolivia last night.

Carol stifles a laugh, still looking at Frank as Jackie grabs her bag.

Be good, Jackie says. And if you can't be good be safe.

Frank reddens as Jackie leaves them.

You weren't here Tuesday, says Frank. Not like you.

Ah, I was hours in the solicitors.

Ah, right. Sorry.

Stop. I wasn't.

He hands her the cash and the slip.

Just that Carol.

Not getting too many bets for that one, she says.

Carol looks again at the slip.

Have you an extra zero on this one Frank?

I know yeah.

OK. Two hundred so.

Frank places the fifties, one after another, into her soft hands.

Have you any others there, Frank?

No, that's me. I'll see you later.

Slip in hand, he shuffles back to his place on the terrace.

Devin's hands work the baggie inside his pocket. A little taster for himself, he reminds himself of Salvo's words, and he sucks his teeth and his gums go numb, go into some kind of perfect nothing, his tongue too, and all the lights switch on in his wiring, and he loves its savage purity. His brain sprints to later, when he's out of here and out for the night. He knows he can fuck. He's been getting sugary confirmation for years now, since he got his dick sucked in a room full of his cousin's mates. He comes back to the job at hand. He'd been talked through it earlier. Nothing to it, Salvo had said. They had a window, a gap Devin can squeeze through, before the cameras are trained on them. Now Devin puts on gloves and the stretched thin rubber feels wrong on his skin. Sauna Winks has his mouth open. Devin stoops down, one knee brushing short wet grass, and works quickly. He keeps one hand on the dog throughout, a reassuring pat turned to a clamp. His other hand dips into the baggie and at the same time he whispers to the dog. He works his fingers until they are where he needs them, at the wrinkly tight orifice at the back of the dog, then a sharp push through and he inserts the finger, powder on, into the dog's hole. Sauna Winks' big eyes snap wider. There's a horrible sucky pull off the hole as he tries to take his finger back, like for a minute his finger is part of the dog. He will spend years trying to run this off. Devin thinks of a line he heard watching the fight last week. All fighters leave something of themselves in the ring. He strips the gloves off, to be shoved in a bin, and he stands up. He was as fast as Salvo told him to be. He looks up. Salvo is where he said he would be. Devin promises himself he will never do that again.

In the parade ring each of the six dogs is stood with its owner in a brilliant blue coat down to its knees. Devin watches this da and his son, then just the son, eating his bar. The state of him in the da's jacket, like a four-foot penguin. He's about the age Devin was when he lost his name. He thinks of his da's line about a shit footballer: that lad wouldn't get a kick in a stampede. Devin misses his da and the things he'd say, misses him every day, a wound with no closing.

Trap One, Majestic Shannon, says the PA. In trap two, Sauna Winks, three is Breakfast Roll, in four Kylemore Wonder, in five Same Bat Channel and in six Charity Maggie. Shane and Jayden stand beside Breakfast Roll. The coats come off the dogs. The hydraulic jaws of the traps bang open.

Jayden rubs and pats Breakfast Roll. The trainers start loading their dogs in, some more willing than others.

You do it, Shane says.

Jayden whispers and cajoles Breakfast Roll towards the trap, clamped between his thighs. Roll loaded, the two of them step away, the dogs' tails going ninety in their traps. The traps clang shut, and the handlers hurry back across the green.

Race ya, Shane says and he takes off and Jayden breaks into a grin and sprints after and he catches up, his body stretching out. They're the first of the trainers to get across to infield. Beside them Keith plays with the zip on his jacket, his hair flicking up away from him.

Horrible seconds, waiting for the bell. Frank clutches his slip and keeps his eyes on the track. The entire stadium is fixed on the race to start, their eyes sucked into the unfolding. Shane brings his hand down onto his son's shoulder. Jayden stuffs the silvery chocolate wrapper into his pocket and stares as the hare tracks along its determined curve, agonizing and inevitable. At the bell the wild orange of the hare flies and the dogs bolt off in hot pursuit. The snap of the race, hind legs flashing away and all of them going bright in floodlit halcyon, a tearing blur over sand.

From the start it's Kylemore Wonder, says the PA, and Shane and Jayden lean into the track and their hopes rise as one.

The dogs round the first bend, low and hard to the ground, and Breakfast Roll is there or thereabouts.

But Kylemore Wonder coming up on a length and a half—Frank closes his fist tight over the slip and urges his chosen dog on and as if listening to the man, Breakfast Roll hauls and scraps himself up into third. A harried whip of motion when Sauna Winks catches Kylemore's leg, catches another, and then it's chaos – a frenzy of hind limbs at sick angles – the two dogs smash and bundle each other up as they hit the sand in an ugly scramble. The crowd gasps and Keith sees his dog smack the ground. Sauna Winks hops back up and rights himself, his race gone but nothing broken. The rest of the dogs scream around the second bend, a lancing motion under sharp-defined light as the race bursts in change, and Breakfast Roll is free of the pack and away by a head. Meanwhile Kylemore Wonder is left far behind, hopping on the sand with his front foreleg gone flappy. Keith's sprinting for the track. His wronged dog tries to hop along without the leg but everyone can see it will never take weight again. The animal is in agony and makes a sound that was with them forever.

There's four dogs left in the race and Breakfast Roll's out by two lengths—

Everyone's roaring, exhortations and curses and the clamour rises, the stadium one great mouth in a crescendo from last bend right along the home straight, the roar mounting and building on itself as it swells to its fullest most feverish pitch.

It's between Breakfast Roll and Majestic Shannon and Breakfast Roll won't be caught he's away!

And down the terrace Frank can see this will be his race and he can hardly believe his luck.

Breakfast Roll the winner from Majestic Shannon and a distant third Sauna Winks.

Jayden leaps seeing it. Shane pumps his fist, justified, and hugs his bouncing son tight into him. The hare shoots into the escape and the dogs canter on past.

What about that? Shane shouts.

He did it!

He did and all.

And his son jumps again. The two of them bounce over to the winner's enclosure, where the winner's sheet is placed over the victorious Breakfast Roll.

Who's the best dog? Jayden asks him as they collect their winner.

Beside the photographer stands her husband, a man of sixty-six, made of liver spots and stray hairs and known only as Tito. From the wife's pocket, the yelpy squeak of a plastic toy and Breakfast Roll's ears shoot straight up at the silly sound and the camera clicks. She shows Jayden the toy and winks at him, a magician revealing her tricks. They're glad-handed and whisked into position, suddenly a crack and they're flashbulbed into blinding nothing, and the nothing stays white and blank, and gradually Shane's vision fades back to him, and he sees his own hand appearing on his son's shoulder, as if returned to him from a bleached pool. He looks at his other hand and realizes he is holding a novelty cheque for five grand.

Frank's beaming as he makes his way down the wide cement steps towards the bookies. His view is blocked by a couple of punters so he's almost there when they part and he sees only Jackie left by the railing, blowing on her coffee. He is still holding his slip out in front of him as his feet slow to a zombie plod and Jackie spots him.

You only just missed her Frank. Here, I'll do it for you. Frank hands over the slip and when she sees it, Jackie's mascara-hyped eyes widen in surprise.

You had him in the last one? Fair fucks.

Every dog, hah. No hundreds now Jackie.

Wouldn't do that to you Frank, she says as she counts out the notes.

Thank you.

There you are, couple of monkeys for you, and the rest in fifties, fourteen hundred in all.

Frank takes his winnings and smiles faintly back.

Some night, Jackie says.

It's up there alright. See ya Jackie. God bless.

He carefully folds away his winnings into his wallet, the most he's won in years, since the big nights. He turns towards the exit, crushing the dead slips underfoot.

In the trainers' yard, dog man lights a smoke and watches the shit go down, another trainer carrying his maimed dog over to Salvo. Salvo is the man to talk to in these sorry situations and dog man knows how it plays out but it is always new for the trainers. This lad is no different, he's been put somewhere else by it, detonated by what's happened. Salvo does the talking and dog man does the driving and it suits both men this way. Salvo has the heavy respect of an undertaker as he tells Keith not to worry about sorting him out tonight, that he's had enough bad news for one night, and he gives Keith his number. A terrible thing, they agree. One snapped leg and another broken hock. There's no coming back from that. Keith lifts his whimpering Kylemore Wonder into the cage, lays him down on blankets and bends down and watched by others he says goodbye to his dog. He hates this, in front of the rest of them, where it should not be. He remembers him as a pup, his big eyes and his waggy tail that never stopped. He presses his forehead into the dog's short bristly hair. He whispers to him what a good dog he is and that he is sorry. Then he closes the door of the cage over on him. He steps away, his hands lost and his jaw clenching and he nods to the bigger man and dog man shuts the door. Keith lets a breath shudder out and dog man gets into the cabin and turns the key and the ignition growls. He sees Keith in his rear-view watching him leave the track with his dog.

All good? Salvo asks Devin.

Yeah.

Salvo tells him well done and stuffs rolled notes into his hand. Devin heads off, fuck watching the rest of it. He whips out the phone to see who's round tonight. Amber, or Aminah maybe. He's in a few DMs at once and he stays online waiting for who replies first. He wants to be done with his name. He had his own name once, had his name to himself. Then his da fucked off on them. His da just started over. Started all over again a few estates over, just started a new life for himself, like nothing had happened, like they didn't exist. Worse, his da went and gave his new son his name too, got himself a new Devin. Devin's half-brother with his full name living less than a mile away. So Devin is weighing his options up. He could pick anything and he is out here, on the grind, making ends and he can see himself in the future.

Maguire swallows the serrated last lump of his steak. Hazel gave hers a good go, only the snaking rind of fat left on the plate. She reaches for her clutch and he knows she's looking for the jacks and he leans back to point the way. She thanks him and he waits a few seconds then turns to watch her arse shift in her white jeans as she walks. You could fill the restaurant with what she doesn't know about all of it. He said he'd given up on these last few stragglers and this is why, nights like this. One good line and you could be getting proper money, litters whelped and their muck shipped all the way to Australia after the manipulating, a nice word for wanking off a greyhound. He knew there were stud dogs with a thousand pups sired off them. It was all lineage. There's only a second or two between first place and the ditch. They don't all make it to the stud book. Maguire never minded seeing another man lose, makes him tick. Gets up in the morning for it. He feels eyes on him and there's Salvatore, just in, the doors still swinging behind him. He stays there, a respectful distance and Maguire nods back at him. This is enough. Long ago he told Salvatore he had no interest in the details. He doesn't want to know about who his Scrote of the Month is or what the buzz is like downstairs. It is quick and quiet when Maguire pays him off. It happens not far from here, but weeks from now, on another night, through revolving glass doors and coffee in a hotel lobby. It is the same hotel, the Mercer at Grand Canal Dock, that Maguire has in mind for later. He can get a room there at short notice. He eyes Hazel on her way back from the jacks. Tonight is exactly what he doesn't need. Complications mean later nights and more to clean up. But that is always the danger, you have to walk around with it, and hope it never comes to that. But it has come to pass now. No rest for the wicked and he wouldn't have it any other way.

When Shane sees Keith, his cousin just raises an open palm to him. Shane is thankful for this. He has made things easy for Shane. Keith will not come over now and Shane will not have to commiserate with him. Shane turns to Jayden to give himself something to do. He feels a debt to Keith he cannot repay, for granting him this, a clemency he does not deserve. He will talk to him another night. Shane wants his son out of here now. An older feeling, as shame and guilt mix and tangle. Breakfast Roll ambles along, pink gums and teeth, but Jayden might float home. They are just at the van when Salvo is suddenly beside them and Shane feels himself tense up.

Congrats lads, says Salvo.

Thanks.

Delighted are ya?

We are indeed, Shane says, we've had some great nights with him.

One great night, Jayden says.

Come here, get him home.

Good luck.

Here's one for you, have a think bout the twelfth, Salvo says, and he's gone.

They pack Breakfast Roll away, Jayden still congratulating him, and Shane drills into himself, inside the bad things in his bad head, his worthless win and his son beside him. He wants them gone from the dirty arena. You've stolen that soon dead dog off your own cousin, is all he can think. A thief in the family, there was nothing worse, and he is the thief.

Once he's buckled up, Jayden asks can they go chipper and Shane is powerless to say no. Ten minutes later they step into Iannelli's. Leaning across the counter is an older gent, the bulb of Marcello Lippi in a Dubs cap, gabbling away in Italian with gusto and great waves of his hands. Taking Jayden here, Shane thinks, add it to the list of things he's got wrong, but this is a special night for the lad, he's allowed chips to top it off. Going past all these somewheres in the van, the stark sting of vinegar is everywhere in the cabin as Jayden shakes out the last of the brown paper bag and Shane lowers his window. The great slugs of the new towers grow every week, leaving Boland's Mills dwarfed underneath, and

158 · DAVE TYNAN

Shane drives on, through town glittering with hotels as his son shines with their triumph. Shane hears his uncle in his head from years before, telling him again, you always remember your first winner.

Carol hugs herself in the cold and wishes she still smoked. She is glad and proud she gave up, but sometimes a gnaw turns up all the same. She's bone tired. Only a few weeks ago Jackie told her what was happening to girls in town now, getting jabbed with needles. Syringes in the club. They remember nothing and wake up far from home. Spiked is right, Jackie had said. Carol shivers at the thought. Her face hadn't felt a fist in three years, and she looks forward to him arriving. It was Jackie put her up to it.

Not gonna lie to you he's not a looker, Jackie had said.

Is he decent?

Jackie squealed at the question and Carol aged about a year.

What's decent? You're gas. Just go.

On his way out, Frank sees Carol. She's checking her phone and he can only keep walking over to her and their mouths both open at the same time. She looks uneasy and he hates that. He would not have her upset, ever.

Frank, she says. Congrats!

Got lucky, he smiles. Have to go spend it now.

There's a little silence and Frank opens his mouth again but they both hear the sound of feet slapping the ground and then Salvo appears, trotting up to the two of them and Frank sees it all as Salvo puts a hand to Carol's elbow.

Sorry I'm late, Salvo says to her.

You're grand, Carol says. This is Salvatore, Frank.

The two men shake hands.

Think I've seen you before, Salvo says to Frank.

Here most nights, for my sins.

Frank just hit the jackpot there, says Carol.

Breakfast Roll? Good spot, thought I was the only cunt who had him.

Anyways, have a good night, Carol. And nice to meet you.

Pleasure. Mind yourself Frank.

Frank takes himself off. Outside the women and the placards are gone. He walks down the street, gone quiet this late. He starts to hate himself in a way he knew he would keep. The Irishtown House is hot and busy, the windows smeared and dripping with condensation as he comes in and sees Tom at the end of the bar. Tom barely lifts a finger to the barman, who sets to work pouring, and Frank sits beside Tom and for the next couple of hours their backs make the same humped pair they did on the terrace.

At home Jayden tells the tale of it and Dee's smile grows as he explodes the yet young story into legend. Shane pulls a can out of the fridge and enjoys the icy bite in his grasp as Jayden takes Dee through each bend, the story much longer than the race was. Jayden keeps rabbiting on to her as she hooshes him up the stairs to bed. Shane looks out into the dark garden as the laughter leaves. He listens to her putting him to bed and after a while Shane knows she won't be coming back down. He is left in the low-lit room alone. He stays up with his family long gone to sleep and drinks the rest of the cans in the fridge. He wakes on the couch in the middle of the night and drags himself up to their marriage bed. He was on thin ice with himself after that.

Now dog man pilots the van through the night, through the Port Tunnel and up the M1. He rolls the window down. He has not turned the radio on since Salvo threw him the keys five years ago. He hears the whimpers of the dog in the back and they are in the north of the county, mist in the fields and pylons in the distance as he takes the turn off the Skerries Road. They are long out of town now, headed in the direction of Swords and Lusk, these quiet parts with bold names, Man O'War and Strifeland. Only the sound of the dog in the back. He prefers not knowing their names.

When dog man parks, he leaves the lamps on, so piercing tunnels of light throw deep into the inky field. He makes a soft sound out his nose as he goes round to the back and opens the doors and in the gloom is the dog, crouched and shivery in the corner of the cage. With one shovel hand he pushes aside rough blankets and scratches Kylemore Wonder behind the ears, where the tags are. He lifts him and carries him further into the field. They come to the place that dog man has decided for them, a hole he dug days ago, before he knew the dog that would go in it. He is firm with the dog underneath him and opens his jacket and pulls out the .22 and grips the walnut stock of the carbine and bends down, close to the panting animal. The sound grows in the human bone cage. The dog's rotten breath rises through his senses as he raises gun to skull. They breathe in unison, in and out, in and out, soft and heavy, until the shot cracks the quiet and drops the dog, flops him down into the soil and with his Leatherman out of its pocket, dog man lowers himself to it and pulling one taut, then the other, he roughly saws off the ears and with the ears, the evidence they bear. There is work in it. He folds the blade back in on itself and stuffs the ears into his pocket. He will burn them later in the barrel in the yard. He will burn his kaks too. When he is finished, he stands alone in the field, above and below what he has done.

AND THE BALLROOM

Outside Arrivals, the tourists looked up at the lashing to fall. Inside, his first five-finger discount in years, swiping the bottle of airport water: start thinking like her. How'd she ever put up with all the airports, Paul kept asking himself as he followed in his sister's steps through Departures. Ash would be the first one you'd pull at security, Ash with her emerald city eyes and hair with its own plans for the evening. She took him to festivals and let him sit in their camp circle, Paul looking between their Hallowe'en faces, laughing with them half the time and laughing to himself the rest, happy as a clam and dumb as a mule. No one was more full of gas fury than Ash: first to pounce, she hated quick and easy, a sudden pure burn on whatever caught her wrath, leaving lads scarred for life with one climbing eyebrow. That night it was losers with too many festival wristbands that wound her up. I'll go round with a scissors, she kept screaming in the lit rain, that's the least I'm cutting off these creeps. Roaring together with the main stage below and the dark valley exploding into view, a negative of a dancing city, insects drawn to a giant ball of light. The next morning and the muck of the campsites after, a kid sprawled across an inflatable, braying to his fallen brethren, lads I can't believe it's over. Over those years Paul grew to agree with his sister: music was better than everything.

He was carried along by the shuffling current towards the gates for the six-twenty flight and he yawned into line, everyone in holiday twos and threes. People used to dress up for flights, his dad had said last night. He could hear the two of them back in the gaff now. See if life has put some manners on her yet, his dad said too, but he looked sorry after he said it and his mam just looked away. Paul did not miss the screaming sessions between the three of them, before their mam left home for the guts of a year. She moved back in but by then Ash had started not coming home.

It was Friday and he wasn't in work. The email factory – writing copy, guilting people into signing online petitions – would still be there when he got back. A day off from finding crisitunities in the morning so the concerned public can help the world over lunch, in between their ASOS tabs. He was in the business of providing conscience balms for office workers. Emails aren't change, he knew that now, and imagine he ever thought different. The email factory had raised proper cash off Brexit and any slow week, bees always worked. Add Your Name, Save the Bees.

You can't see into another skull for as long as a song. She'd left him everything, either way. Before she vanished, his sister's scowls were the best teachers he ever had. Other lessons came for free in her wake. She used to take him everywhere, wide-eyed and tagging along, and he never knew why, never saw what was in it for her, and he got to know her fella Lorcan and their mates better than his own. Lorcan was like a big brother. Maybe it amused her that their parents thought going out with her was the safer option, as if his sister protected him from the worst rather than led him right to it. Dead venues now, all of them knocked last year and maybe

just as well. He was starting to notice anyone his own age still
lost in the dark. Last year in District 8 a child had bounced up
to himself and Danny. Her button face had made him think
of a Bratz doll, a glittery baby raver reaching for his ear.

Hey! You selling?

No. I'm just old, he said.

Sold? Like sold out?

Old! I'm just old!

Oh my God, sorry. Have a good one yeah!

Danny breaking his hole beside him as she peeled off.

Don't even fancy them anymore, Danny said.

What happened back then. Everything that came before was
only the shallows. Ash was the one who found Lorcan face
down and non-responsive. After that, everything that relaxed
her stressed her parents. Reconciled, they were too polite to
despair at any volume. By the time they were angry she was
gone and they were only sad about her now. When she'd first
left a city on its knees, he'd held the fort at home. She'd said
something's very fucked if you can't get a gang out on a Friday.
He always remembered her five steps ahead of him, hunting
down trouble. He hadn't seen her in two years now but he
could still see her lip ready to curl. She looked like Fairuza,
the girl out of The Craft, the same one from Return To Oz.
She loved Return To Oz. She never came home. Her old email
was hopeless, just a place he left questions piling up. At the
gate everyone had priority boarding and he followed the hen
parties across the tarmac. It was September and freezing on
the steps up. Her birthday was the twenty-first of last month
and he wondered how she'd spent it. Not like her old ones
maybe. What had they left for themselves back in the gore of
the past. Everyone has their reasons but might help to know
more of them. His sister might still be trapped in the mirror.

He'd only told his parents that he had an idea. He thought they'd be happier about it. Maybe talking to a bar on facebook that knows your daughter wasn't the present he'd thought it was. He told them nothing about her belly. He had worried they'd started putting her to rest in their heads after two years. Pass on grief. Throw it down the family tree to strike the next monkey and start them falling through the branches. Stick the runt on the plane, sure you're not doing anything else. His phone buzzed. An image from Danny, an old CD cover of peasants dancing, their skirts hiked up. The title read Come Dance With Me In Ireland.

– Can't

– You can yeah

Danny helped him get here, but his mate's memory was a patchy thing. He'd donated a decent portion of his brain to the dark web, a giddy guinea pig to whatever came in the post. He dropped a pin for Danny by way of explanation and watched the map zoom and lurch down.

– Shit sorry. Forgot

– Talk to you on the other side

– Good luck with your sis

– Thanks

When she made the mistake and let him in on it, when out of nowhere the photo popped up on his feed. He'd been half scrolling, half asleep but he'd managed a screenshot of it. She'd stuck it up then whipped it down a few minutes later. Maybe she had to tell someone. Maybe whoever was around wasn't enough. He didn't have a clue anymore. She was self-ish before she was a mother. This was just the latest, most selfish act yet, the end level boss of her looking after number one. But she couldn't be number one anymore. For the hundredth time he looked at the screen grab again. She must have been looking somewhere else just before it was taken. She was smiling and with child. The caption read, I blame this place xx. He'd only needed the where, and someone took it so there was a who. He zoomed in on her cradled stomach. There must be another human crawling around now, or not crawling but alive, crying and watching. That night he paced the kitchen with the news. He'd thought Danny would be up late and he was right and they'd gone back and forth over it.

– Not exactly the Uighurs is it Paolo?

– What?

– They're disappearing graveyards. We're keeping tabs on a genocide bro.

– Send me a link. What bout the picture of her?

– You don't need chronolocation

– What's that mean

– Looks like Lisbon

The next morning he'd woken to nineteen consecutive messages from Danny, the last one a little after five, a googlemap of the bar from her photo. He'd written her a letter, pages and pages, ripped it up and just posted off a note instead, addressed to the bar, with every way she could get in touch. Months later he got a text in work.

– Paulie! It's ya missing sister

– How you?

– Stall it

He'd booked flights on his lunch. The steward looked tired under the hairnet, but her face was a brazen terracotta as she told him to turn off his phone before take-off.

A rush of heat straight off the plane and the train was seventies orange and brown and it dipped underground and carried him into the city. He surfaced from the metro blinking into the day and looked around a huge empty square. Everything bounced in his eyes. He shouldered his rucksack and scurried for shade. Overhead wires split the sky above the tram lines. Everything was at an angle as he sweated gamely down the sloped street, the cobbles nobbly and curved under his runners. You're on your holidays, he told himself, and he wished he could believe it. A clear cerulean day and suddenly he wanted to be here with someone, holding hands and saying the names of shops and restaurants aloud to each other, just arsing round with nothing to do and all day to do it. Wrought-iron balconies above him and hectic aerials jostling on top of houses like nests of mad hair. She never gave herself a minute. He was never as funny as her but the funniest people he knew were hardest on themselves so maybe he was better off with less to say. Her kind were soft sound lunatics. She'd slogged it out in a call centre in Melbourne for the first few months, twenty-eight dollars an hour which was class and everything else which wasn't. They didn't understand me, she'd said. He'd never gone out, only saw them in photos, the lads they were warned about from the estates at home, lads with their jaws set on making a fortune selling to the rest of them. Half the heads she was running from were already over there waiting and she dove right in. Hanging off the upside-down world. No word then for ages. She told a friend who told him she'd disappeared herself out of Europe, working in the same chain of hostels from Argentina to Brazil, running bars that never closed, a few years older than the revolving door of backpackers. He'd seen some of that himself but he didn't miss cold showers, sleeping on benches or getting kicked off trains at dawn. It was all rushing back as he found the hostel, still pumping sweat in reception. He was face to face with a brassy receptionist who thought this was his first time away and he wanted to tell her that she'd been nowhere and knew nothing, but he just went mumbly as he took the key and hiked up the stairs. He'd got a private room. Gone bougie now, he could hear her sneer. Bag off, he charged his phone and spreadeagled on the bed. He changed into shorts and felt the relief of air round his shins. He leaned out the window: the sky a total azure and chattering kids below. He went downstairs, through the kitchen, past some drama amongst some French teenagers by the open fridge and out into the stone garden full of wizened trees. The bar beyond had little seats on fluorescent astroturf. He wondered if she ever got sick of being surrounded by students. He bought a euro beer in a tiny beaker then another and watched a loose-shirted ponytailed man talk greasy to two English girls. Look at this prick. Never trust a man in white jeans. He took in the necklaces and wide leather wristbands on the man as he explained things to the girls. A forty-something full moon creep.

I've been in your country, the man told the girls.

In the late morning he climbed up through the streets of Alfama, nearly squealing in the midday sun. His calves burned and he was regarded by old men shrunk in the shade, silver chest hair stealing out of their pristine white shirts, sun-faded things like postcards never sold. Up at the mirador the glary city spread out and swooped down to the river. On a dazzling white wall, graffiti read You Will Never Be A Local. He agreed and when no one was looking he took a picture of it. The flea market was too hot and his head was melting. He sat down in the nearest little restaurant he could find. His sweat dropped onto his plate of crusty bread and sardine paste. A table over, a fly buzzed over glistening pork fat. Back in the hostel he flopped down and napped. He woke two hours later to heat and ceiling, sluggish and drowsy. Still a pure proud blue out the window. The communal shower helped and he washed looking out the tiny window at the roofs. When he turned the shower off, he saw a human shit near his feet. He stepped over it. He could see himself back in work, lying about where he stayed.

The river whiffed up foul and hugged the city. He stepped up onto the clattertram behind a Japanese family and rocked along. He went underground at Baixa-Chiado, a bustling whale belly of a station. Off the train, he surfaced into a wide open square then followed the narrowing lanes past the cafés.

Finally, he stood outside the bar. It was a tiny spot, even smaller than the picture had suggested, just the bar, a corridor leading off it, and four tables. There were no customers. Paul stepped inside. He saw a striking man in his thirties leaning on the high wooden counter tapping into a laptop. He'd a full head of sable-dark hair and a neat beard, deep sun-filled skin against a dark green t-shirt that showed his arms, inked and lined like ogham. When he looked up, Paul straightened up. The man smiled and came out from behind the bar, a towel over his shoulder.

I'm supposed to meet someone here, Paul said.

Yes, you are, he said. Not me.

His friendliness disarmed Paul.

I'm in the right place so.

Yeah. She looks like you.

Sorry?

Maybe is the ears, the man said, cocking his head to look at Paul from a new angle.

We're like a pair of elephants, Paul said. Least she's got the hair to cover it.

The man laughed.

I'm Lucas.

Paul.

Paul put his hand out but Lucas spread his arms and Paul was enclasped in a big bear hug. His clean strong aftershave swam up Paul's nose and made him think of lagoons. He made sense to Paul.

OK, she wants you to meet her here, Lucas said, lifting a map from the counter that he'd already marked up. He walked him out onto the street and pointed the way, placing a hand on his shoulder.

It's not far. Maybe five minutes.

Paul thanked him and set off. It was dead hot in the square and he felt sick. He saw her first, sitting at a table outside a small café. She wasn't pregnant. She turned his way, saw him and hopped up out of her chair. He could barely believe he was walking towards her. There were times before she was too thin. Not now. She looked healthy. He could tell them that much at home. She just held her arms out.

Hey Paulie, she said.

Hey Ash, he said.

Give us a squeeze.

They grasped each other in a deep hug and sat down. She ordered imperials for the two of them, tiny ice-cold glasses of beer and he sank half of his in one go and she grinned and judged him for it. He was amazed how dark she was this close. He checked her arms for new tats but saw nothing past the old lines. They both leaned back.

Lisbon so, he said.

Yeah. There was a reason.

She leaned in to him, dead serious.

It's just. I have a problem.

She placed a hand on his wrist, brown on pasty white.

An addiction. I can call it that now.

OK.

I'm just a hoor for tiles, she said.

Fuck off.

Ash brayed. Paul shook his head.

You're in the right spot so, he said.

Yeah, think so.

There's a museum for the tiles, you not been?

Nah I was waiting for you.

Nice one.

They went quiet. It was too early to ask her anything.

Thanks for coming, she said.

Thanks for summoning me.

He caught a strange look in her eyes – a gap he could dive through – and he went for it.

Can I meet him so?

Her eyes shot open, snared. She swore softly and twisted, looking over her shoulder and out at the sunny square like they might be watched by spies.

Or her?

Stop Paul.

I don't know do I?

You saw the picture?

Yeah, he said. Well, that was the plan wasn't it?

I don't know. There wasn't much plan to things. He's a him, she said.

His sister looked away then, blinking her eyes into wet glass.

Whose is he? he said, and saw straight away it was completely the wrong thing to say.

Fuck off, his sister said.

Sorry.

You wouldn't ask that if you'd met him.

Sorry.

He's mine. Prick.

I said sorry.

Duarte.

Duarte?

Yeah. Course you can meet him, Ash said. You don't get a choice.

She brightened even as her lip wobbled. She left some coins on the table and they stood and left the sun-blasted square. He followed her through the warmed streets single file on the narrow path and when it widened, she stepped to his right.

Let me go this side, she said.

The hot steep climb took them up past banana yellow houses before she stopped at an old apartment block. She had to shove the heavy door until it opened. She went up the musty staircase and he climbed behind her as his eyes adjusted to the gloom.

They're hounding grannies out, Ash said. They turn off the electricity on them.

Happens at home too.

Not like here.

He didn't argue. She let them in and he looked up at high ceilings. She went ahead, slung her bag off and dropped keys onto the kitchen table. Crimson-coloured throws over a slouchy couch and a huge tapestry covered the wall. Paul reeled. The only plastic in the room was the toys scattering the rug in brash primary colours.

Nice spot, he said, looking around for who else lived here.

It's a chaotic harmony baby, she said, hamming it up for him in a cheesy Portuguese accent as she tied her hair up in sharp twists.

Paul stepped closer to a collection of photos, of their parents when younger, and their mam's sixtieth. A squawk from deeper within the flat. Paul swung towards the kitchen, looking inside it and beyond but he didn't see a child. He saw the man from the bar. Lucas.

You were at the bar, Paul said.

Yeah, I teleported, Lucas said, a wolfish crack to his smile. Fair play.

It's my bar, he said. Maybe I have lost . . . two customers? Ash looked between them. Lucas disappeared and returned with a baby in his arms and Paul only had eyes for the child. The boy had the skin of his father, a rich pecan, and the perfect black hair of both parents. He took Paul in, then started cawing up at him, the child creasing himself, apeshit with delight.

That's your uncle big man, Ash said. Paul, meet Duarte.

Nice to meet you, Duarte.

Paul wanted to hug him, tighter and harder than could be safe.

Here's your nephew, Lucas said.

Lucas passed him over to Paul. He took the child into his arms and Paul was shocked at how sturdy he was. He was all look. He seemed unsure now, then lit up again. Paul couldn't get close enough. This charming boglin and how quickly the weather changed on his face. He wanted to smell him and nuzzle him forever. He was only pure things, everything new, nothing hidden and nothing yet known, everything for the first time.

The smile just bursts in him, he said.

Paul's arms were shaking and he was suddenly scared to hold him.

Jesus might drop him.

I got you, Lucas said and took the child back.

Paul caught Duarte's big curious eyes in Lucas' arms. Strange sounds escaped the baby's mouth.

It's grand, Paul said. Can I have him back?

Lucas went back into the kitchen. Paul sensed his sister's eyes on him. He sat down on the rug with the baby in front of him, who gabbled happily to himself in some kind of frog language, placeholders for future words. He clambered for everything and Paul passed toys to him. Baby Duarte used the dainty fingers of his pudgewad hands to try stuffing each toy into his mouth.

Everything goes in the gob, Ash said.

She sat him up on the back of the deep couch, his thunder thighs going ninety with furious kicking.

It's mad, he only kicks when he's wrecked, she said.

Paul couldn't take his eyes off him.

Seven months next week, Ash said.

Duarte stilled and blinked, three hundred percent awake, sucking it all into his understanding, racing everything in front of him into his eyes.

Here, I've bottles to do. You OK with him for a minute?

Yeah sure.

Ash went into the kitchen. Just the two of them. His hair was madly awisp, but there was no doubt he was a Portuguese boy. So much is already decided. His nephew had been kept from him. His baby otter paws rested on his barrel belly. Paul wanted to grab him again, for all of them, for his parents who had no knowledge of the boy's existence. Paul heard his sister in the other room, this new mother he knew, and he felt a flashing anger. There was a cruelty outside this room, that was nothing to do with this room, in them not knowing any of it, and he saw his parents rattling around the gaff, ignorant of this font of life coursing through the world. A curdling rose in him as he realized what he had been denied, what had he already missed of this little life that he would not get again. Seconds minutes hours lost. What strange blinks and unknowable looks from his nephew were already gone and missed and it snarled in him. Nothing they ever did to her was as cold as this. Not even close. Ash came back in and cooed and lifted Duarte up and he pummelled her in joy and hid in her breast. Lucas appeared, apologetic at the door.

Sorry. I have to bring him to Avó Ana, he said.
Lucas placed the infant in a sling and promised to meet them at the bar later. Paul kissed Duarte on the forehead and watched the door even after it had clicked shut.

Back down in the blaring bright, outside seemed too much. Paul took a few steps away and craned his head back and regarded the beautiful crumbling building where his nephew lived.

You've to tell them, he said.
Ash screwed her face up and made herself busy checking her bag.

Ash. They don't fucking know they're grandparents. They'll lose their minds.

You didn't tell them?

No I fucking didn't. I didn't know. And fuck off. That's not my job.

There's no jobs in it, she shouted.

I didn't fucking have him, did I?
She took that and ran a hand through her massive hair and shook it back. She lit a smoke.

Now what? he asked her.

Let's go to the beach.

They got the train out and walked past dusty scrapland and bare concrete and then their feet sank into hot sand, the air fragrant after the brine of the river. She had boys' shorts on. He always thought she barely looked Irish. At the water's edge she marched ahead of him, picking up pace, almost running, a halting charging as the water got higher and then she dove and vanished under. He followed, slower and only committed when his balls stung with the cold. He gulped and launched himself into the next wave and burrowed and tunnelled through the ocean, then lifted and broke back up, eyes lamped shut and her laughter in his ears. For a moment, blinking, he couldn't see her, only undulating waves and blinding sun. Then he saw her. Further out, she bobbed like a seal in silver. She stayed out for an eternity, past the rolling pitch and triangle clashes of the tinfoil sea.

Back drying on the beach, the netting of his togs was cutting into him. He was crouched over, scratching himself.

You alright there? she asked him.

It's my internet, he said, rearranging himself.

Join the fucking club, she barked.

She started laughing and he looked over.

We'd make a good pair. Arse Rash and Sand Vag, she said. Like Sharky and George, solving crimes up and down the beach.

The ocean before them. He took a picture as the sun set, trying to sneak her in on the edge of his shot.

Subtle, she chided, dodging out of frame and lighting another smoke. He sent a picture of the beach and turned his phone off. Ash went off and came back with cans and they sat cross-legged opposite each other in the heat. They hungrily dug into hours of home. They named the finest pubs. The lure remained while around them American accents cut the soft slosh of waves. Ash yawned like a lion and they collected themselves and left the beach as the blare of sun left the day. They made their way to a table of a beachfront restaurant. He read the laminated menu.

Snails, he said. You can get full dose or half dose.

You're a full dose, she said.

But she went somewhere else, looking out to sea, lost in the horizon.

I'll leave you maps, she said.

You're very good.

No stress pal.

D'you ever miss home? he asked.

No. It wouldn't be what it was anyway, she said.

Don't worry it's not.

How are they?

Mam and Dad?

She chewed the fat of her lip and nodded, stricken before he'd a chance to answer.

Same, he said, I've to keep putting the number up. On what old is. Used to think they were old. But that was years back. What's that make them now?

D'you know what I loved hearing, at funerals? No age. He was no age.

They walked slowly along the beach, brushed by waves receding as evening closed. Back in town they wound down tapering lanes to Lucas' bar. Ash was loud but no louder than normal when the kids at the next table laughed, looking over. Next thing she reared up and they didn't see her coming.

Eu sei que estou a gritar! Estou a ficar surda foda-se!

They all looked like someone had died. She glared at them, one by one, and they apologized in turn. Finally, she turned back to Paul.

Softened their cough for them, she said. Fucking embryos.

She stared back at them, and he quickly put an arm around her to stop her having another go.

Sorry, she said. That was bout me.

They went inside then, through the curtain down the back, into some mad shebeen, close tables and lispy tongues in the deep twilight of a tiny garden, candles winking in alcoves. She looked into him like she never had before.

It's my ears Paulie, she said.

It's your ears, yeah. It's your mouth.

No. My ears.

Your ears.

I'm going deaf y'know.

No.

For years he would swear she only said it the once. She would remember it differently.

No, he said again. No, I don't know.

Deaf, yeah.

Fucking how would I know?

She tapped her right ear.

This one, she said. Definitely this one anyway.

Paul's skin moved around on him. Ash's eyes were full and it only took one blink to set tears running down her cheeks. Then she made awful sounds. She looked smeared and sorry.

Serves me right, she said.

What? Stop it.

I'm going deaf, Paulie. Maybe not all the way deaf but that's a shit maybe.

Freezing spears in him and he couldn't match the icy attack of it with her calm face before him.

There's a bone growing in my ear, she said.

Ash . . .

The doctors don't know. They're useless . . . nah, don't mean that. They're grand. But they can't tell me what's happening.

He flew back through memory snatches: she was always on the same side of him in all of them and it made horrible sense. He realized with cold-water clarity that he just thought she never knew how loud she was, or never cared. It was years and years since he had been embarrassed to go to the cinema with her. She had always walked on the right-hand side of him, looking into the sun. Her face hung before him. The air of the evening lost its hug.

Can you fucking imagine? she said.

No, he blurted.

Every sound was distant and he rubbed his eyes but they were both still here.

No?

No . . . can't imagine. I'm sorry Ash.

Something crept around them then, passed through her and into him.

Jesus we all talk some shite don't we? Paul said.

Yeah.

Mostly bollix.

Yeah, but I love it though, she said. Shite talk was my favourite sound in the world.

He leaned closer to her, thinking she might crack and flood again. They watched laughing young couples make plans to meet again as they left. He smoked one of her fags. She pushed the ashtray across, her face twitched occasionally and they were alone in the garden.

Here, she said, you know when saps ask you, what music d'you listen to?

Yeah. Don't trust anyone who says everything.

If you say everything, you only listen to shite. But what do I fucking listen to? What do I listen to now?

He had no answer. When he put his hand over hers, she let him. She cried first, then the both of them, raggedy hard and they held each other heaving, buried in each other. Messy ugly sobs into each other's hair, and he was stuck in a jungle of her curls and she laughed through the mess and drew a hand across her nose, leaving a thin snail trail of snot glistening on her wrist. He swiped his own eyes and Ash grabbed him up and that set her off too.

They ordered more and they ordered tequila. Everything sped up and softened. He let her rant. He loved her ranting. No one ever did it better.

Last anythings fuck me up, she said, her finger sliding round the rim of her glass.

There was nothing like her real laugh, a 3 a.m. hyena sprung from nowhere, an offering to the night. He never matched it, that sound he had missed the last few years, and he thought that he must know it better than anyone.

D'you know what the worst is? she asked him and he shook his head.

Feel like I'm into tunes like I never was before, she said. Since last year. Like I can't get enough. I . . . grow with it or something. And it's all disappearing. But it was just . . . there, just around, and it was shit, most of it. For ages, shit tunes. And they come on in my head. Lucas keeps saying I should be listening to new things. And maybe he's right but I don't know if I've the time for that. Sometimes I'll listen to one song for days. So I have it.

She fell silent, far off and still. He pictured her in her flat in the dark, trying to make songs hers.

It was . . . she started but her grief gulped her up and mangled it. She concentrated on breathing out, until she could make words again.

It was the smell on the bus, she said. I was on the bus and someone smelled it and moved seats to get away from it. Rotting fucking flesh, like. It reeks. And it was me. It was my ear.

They'd want you to come home, Ash. I mean, they would.

I know yeah.

They'd pay for it. Doctors, whatever.

Yeah, it's not about them anymore.

Think about it.

Maybe.

Yeah?

Maybe next year, she said, staring at the ground. Wasn't sure I could be a good mam, she said. Never mind a good deaf mam. And he's got a granny here. An avó. Not that . . . she's amazing, anyway. Lucas' mam. I mean the two of us can't understand a word the other one says, but I get her.

I should have been here, he said.

She tried to smile but looked like she might burst.

Bollix. You'd other things on, she said.

Not that much.

Anyway, she said, I was flat out being mental. Until everything.

He thought of Duarte's chubby little armbands, the best fat in the universe.

I know, she said. Here, present, she said and pushed an A4 printout across the table at him. He lifted the page and read it aloud.

Nova Batida, he said and pulled his neck back.

She was brimming with mischief.

A festival? he asked and she grinned big and bold.

Half price for residents.

Music art and culture says here, he read aloud.

Don't stress it. We're not going to any talks.

Serious?

Look at the lineup, she said.

I'm looking, he said. I've even heard of some of them.

He could tell she was enjoying this trick, this card up her sleeve.

Tonight, he said.

Yeah. Four Tet headlining.

Can hardly fucking say no, can I?

No. It's decided.

They walked down one street with another street far below, a big red carpet for the tourists, she said. She said she had never set foot in the Time Out Market. They walked in and she took one look at the uniform food court and walked straight out again. On the tram out he watched her through the reflections of the window as her face disappeared into buildings, fractured by sudden slants of light. He wondered what song would be her last, what she would pick or what he would. Rez / Cowgirl. Song to the Siren. Definitely not Enjoy the Silence, anyway. It had to do everything and a song can't do everything any more than a night could.

That's where we're going, she said and pointed at the rust-coloured bridge in the distance.

The bridge?

Under it.

Before Belém he leaned against the glass to get a better look at a huge concrete wave towering over the waterfront. Hard cut stone missionaries with blank eyes staring out to sea. Navigators, priests and princes, with broadswords, crosses and bibles.

Monument to the Discoveries, she said.

Looks mad, he said.

They all left from here, she said. All the lads off to stick some flags in Brazil. Free smallpox with every cross.

They laughed together in the reflection. When they hopped off the tram and walked up the motorway the sun lorded it over them and he choked back the exhaust fumes in his throat, his brain pounding from the heat and Ash striding ahead of him, growing in power as they got closer. He made them eat. They sat outside and ordered wine and fish and it came with charred and blackened scales, sliced spuds swimming in grease.

Will you see them? he asked.

Mam and Dad?

Yeah. Please.

Have to get my head round this first, she said, rapid tapping her smoke.

You can always come home.

Yeah. Kinda. I know.

You're lucky I'm a pushover.

I don't feel too lucky, she said, sullenly watching the oncoming stream of colours and yelps of heads festival-bound.

No way to raise a child, she intoned in their dad's flat midlands accent. They'll think I'm bringing him up in a squat. Playing him jungle instead of reading to him.

You could do both, he said.

Yeah. Cow goes moo, bass goes wob wob wob.

What kinda mam you gonna be?

Her face moved through a few things before she landed on it.

Deaf mam, she said.

Partially deaf isn't deaf.

They won't say partially in the playground. Duarte with the deaf mam.

Maybe kids are getting sounder.

Wouldn't bet on it, Paulie.

The future lack and loss was shuddering through her, shaking her from the shoulders down and he was scared to cut her off or interrupt her.

He's just started laughing. Sunday was the first time.

Paul said nothing.

I know what I'm losing now.

In time he brought her round again with talk of old madness at festivals past, watching the stream of ravers become a river. She left a big tip and followed the likely-looking lads and the women they wouldn't wait for. On the way in they walked through colours and posers and tables full of people eating. They walked between giant warehouses converted into shops and restaurants, under gaping holes in the old factory building. Fake birds hung above, disappearing inside the cratered wall.

There you are now, she said to him in the queue for wristbands, looking at the enormous mural above them, stretching up the side of the warehouse. A huge American Eagle with a pinstriped suit and briefcase frowned down at them.

I'll sniff out the pints, he said. You sniff out the messing.

Grand.

He found the bar and waited amongst their angular English. Extremely London things everywhere, mad patterns on loose shirts: Tony Manero, tropical fruit, the NHS logo above a Nike tick.

That is bang tidy mate, someone was shouting behind him as the track lifted.

Ginola-era Spurs shirts, and bum bags over swimming togs, socks with flip-flops, all younger than them, all bouncing and throwing their heads back, those freaks who got too close to the decks at Boiler Room but here in real life, weirdos incriminating themselves. Ash took it all in like she was witnessing a massacre in real time, giving the crowd the evil eye as he passed her a beer.

Should have known, she said.

What?

They're all Brits! she roared.

She cackled as the looks came in. She smiled back at all of them, a pig in shit. They dropped into it and talked of the Sassenach until his Irish ran out.

Wished I'd more of it, he said.

Me too.

The muffled noise growing towards them and they followed the path made by barriers into the main hall, like stepping through a siege door. They were both plunged back into what light did to smoke. Echoes in the gigantic cavern: there was nowhere like this at home anymore. They were just in time for who she wanted to see, Nubya. He hadn't heard of her. They listened to Lost Kingdoms and she stood beside him, slow swaying to the robed woman on stage as the notes climbed and danced. Ash clapped louder than anyone. Stained-glass chapel light fell on them from above. They went exploring and turned a corner, Til Debt Do Us Part stencilled on the wall ahead, and it was filling up now. They got caipirinhas and she stabbed and mashed the mint like she had something against it. She kept smacking her lips and looking around then she was up and off and floating about. He watched her

run things. He could never do that: land into a group of ran-
domers and just make it hers without anyone knowing or
minding. The gang looked at her like they couldn't believe
their luck and she turned back to Paul with a crafty smirk
and he knew she had it sussed. They called it dizz and told
them to watch out for novocaine, it only numbs, doesn't get
you anywhere. They sat down with them. The soundest lads
were from Sheffield. He thought the lad closest to him introduced himself as groggy.

Froggy mate, Froggy. Here, this will absolutely fry your
weasel.

Cheers.

Things were distributed. The lads said half the big names
had cancelled.

No slowthai, Froggy told Ash.

Is that bad? Ash asked.

Yes mate. He has a Boris head.

He can keep it.

You're brother and sister, Froggy said. That's amazing.

This makes me want to drink an angel, one of the lads
said, staring agog at the bridge, snake-charmed by the tunes,
the crowds and the view. Paul and Ash shared a laugh at the
state of themselves, all the lovely nonsense around them, a
dance at the edge of the world. Ash kissed his temple and
wrapped him up in a headlock. In the jacks he slapped hand-
fuls of cold water on the back of his neck. More things she'd
shown him. Two lads were cracking each other's backs. They
went searching for any hydration.

Shouldn't ever be queues for water, she said.

You got to let the Brits queue. It's their heritage.

Needed that, he gasped minutes later, slugging deep
from the bottle until its ribbed shell crinkled in his hand.

This water shit. Might catch on yet, she said.

Good stuff, yeah.

That'll be the makings of you, she said. Come on, he's on now.

The heatwall bombed them back in, like entering a blast furnace. He couldn't see his hands and he was sweating balls again. Towering gantries stretching into nothing and he knew where they were headed. They snaked through the shadow hall and stopped behind the sound desk. They were all her nights, he never envied her the days. They were always going to be out. She seemed happy. Gorgeous void above and smiles wide strobed back in and out of it, heads swilling upwards, gladdened smirks at a bass line switching, clowning laughing as it rises. When the bass kicks the room back together and everything erupts flamingo pink. Her kind of night. When the whole huge room lit up, then sudden pop after all the mounting machines and they looked at each other in the perfect dark and they both laughed. She was beaming and they sang the old Ne-Yo song together, how they were sick of love songs and tired of tears. The track cut and everyone knew the words, the whole hall singing, and he leaned in to her but it was no use, she couldn't hear, each turn back was more useless and more hopeful til they've nothing left but all of it shining and one.

I wish all of us to return safely and for the Emerald City
and all the people in it to be restored to life.

I can't sleep and I talk about a place that I've been to but nobody believes it exists.

BABY'S FIRST PLAGUE

You could get your eggs frozen, her mother said.
Róisín looked down at the boiled egg in her salad, pale yellow rimmed with ash grey, then back to her mother.

D'you know how much it costs? Róisín said.
This stopped things.
Thousands.
Did you look it up? her mother asked eagerly.
No.
They were saying that some of these big places, they do it for you.
Bet they do.
They'll pay for it.
They'll be paying tax next.
She was three years older than her mother was when her mother had her. Her mother could always tell when Róisín was about to Say Something. Róisín liked the feeling though she wasn't proud of it. Like a royal pickled in gin, worry was the fluid that sustained her mother. She had dodged Sunday dinner the week before so here they were, poking salads in Avoca. Her mother didn't want to know about who owned direct provision centres.

Your father likes the bread.
Róisín said nothing.

And he's right. It's nice bread.

It's not about the bread.

Multi-seed.

Her parents had separated their lives within the house. She still made him his dinner. Róisín looked around, at pert smiling faces, pearl clutchers in pastels, and the few men in gilets. The wallpaper was covered in pink roses and gold frames with nothing inside them. She was watching all the chattering Beatrix Potter women when suddenly she was dive-bombed by a waitress. She flinched and knocked her coffee over everything. They all apologized to each other and cleaned up together as it soaked the leaves of her salad in a watery brown. The waitress had the hamstery features of a child star as she smiled at Róisín.

Can I get you a fresh one?

I'm alright.

You sure?

Yeah, my body produces enough anxiety as it is.

Róisín, her mother scolded, then raised an open palm to the waitress in appeasement.

We're fine, thank you.

The waitress bubbled off and her mother frowned.

She's just doing her job, her mother said.

I know.

Her mother brought up Róisín's ex. The thought of running into him had kept her from a march last week and she hated him for that too. If he was there, she wouldn't be. The things they can take from you can barely be counted. The only person she'd broken up with this year was her counsellor. She knew she should try see more from her mother's side, all she had lived through, all she had told her and all she hadn't. She had her bus pass now and two kids raised, Róisín here and Brian flung foreign and happy, or at least not sniping at her over salads. Her mother picked at West Cork crab. Róisín heard the frantic scurrying inside her chest again. Her mother asked her about Marcus.

It's Manus.

Manus, sorry.

Blessed are the sound co-workers or flatmates who push things towards bearable, and Manus was sixteen stone of Galway kindness and both. He'd moved into the gaff the summer before when Loz moved in with her fella. She'd never lived with just one flatmate before, never mind one she liked: it was almost magically sound. In work, where they'd met, he remained the single soul in the office she felt easy around, and they were keeping each other sane in there.

He's grand yeah.

Could you not cook together some nights?

We drink together some nights?

Her mother made an offended sound.

Well, you could cook while you're at it.

Yeah, and you could get Dad to do the dishes but I'm not holding my breath am I?

Cutlery and whispered tones surrounded them. Róisín saw she had made her mother's face fall.

That night in her room, her phone rang like a scalding. The screen imposed the fact: Gary Landlord. The phone rang and rang and eventually she had to answer it.

Hi Gary.

Hey Róisín. How's the form, now's OK to talk yeah?

She knew it was her turn to speak but she decided to skip it. She could play this waiting game, bleed the chat dry.

You're out of the office, anyway? Gary asked. Don't know

what your plans are. But I shouldn't, should I? I'm not the Stasi ha!

Gary Landlord finished sentences with laughs that encouraged participation. She held on for silence.

Anyway. I know I said I'd be in touch, hoped to be moving on this faster, but here we are. We'd be crazy not to sell now, you know yourself. So just wanted to letcha know. If you can be out two weeks from now, that'd be awesome.

Two weeks?

Yeah, I know. Look, we had an arrangement that suited everyone. Way below market rate.

Gary officially wasn't renting it but he could take cash off them for now.

I mean, all good things come to an end, you know yourself, Gary Landlord said.

He laughed and she said nothing and he kept talking as she looked around the room, at the hill of earrings on her bedside table, at the bare walls and the suitcase on top of the flatpack wardrobe. She started packing it all up in her head. It never took that long. Half a Saturday would remove her from the room, like she was never here. Even as she hung up she could feel herself hyperventilating. She knew Manus kept comedown materials for when he crashed after a rager. She snuck into his room. She then realized she didn't know where to start. The front door opened and she couldn't move.

Heya, Manus called out and she was stuck.

Manus got closer, then opened his bedroom door and Róisín had nothing to say. She crumpled up and slumped against the wall, turning to hide her prickling tears.

Eh, evening hun . . . this isn't your room, Manus said.

Yeah I know. It's not yours either.

Sorry?

He's kicking us out. Gary.

Manus' face softened and he understood then and sneered.

The fucking vermin. He rang?

She could feel the salty wet sliding down her face and Manus stepped into the room.

Yeah, just now. Eh, d'you have anything to calm me down? I'm freaking out.

He hugged her, and she breathed out. He stepped past her then and rooted around in a drawer. Róisín looked around the bigger room. Manus handed her a snapped-off segment of blister pack.

They're proper shit, he said.

Thanks, Róisín sniffled.

Manus went straight to get her a glass. She popped the Xanax out of the foil into the hot clam of her palm. She placed them on her tongue and swallowed down hard. She got into her mooching pants and felt things die down and unclaw, an enveloping comfort, like being wrapped in wool.

I can't start looking, she said. Landlords and their wide-angle lenses. All the rooms look wrong.

In fairness, it allows them to charge obscene rent and thus buy more wide-angle lenses.

True. Just . . . can't be arsed, she said.

Like the Ra told Thatcher, we only have to be lucky once.

Bitch still died of natural causes.

They got pissed on the couch and cursed Gary Landlord, pointing out the shit they'd fixed and paid for themselves and opened another bottle, delaying inevitables.

It was only Tuesday and very February. The election had meant nothing. Town was a weird manacled future, sinkholes appearing out of nowhere and mad new gaps through familiar views. She was glad to see Manus outside the office, wiping crumbs from his baggy shirt.

How was your mam?

Grand. Concerned. Same. What's your afternoon?

He held the door open for her and sang the answer.

Letting the days go by, letting the office hold me down.

Inside they hurried past Lucy the Reception Dragon, mercifully on her phone for once. Manus objected to the name on the basis that you can't have a boring dragon. Anything anyone ordered online had to go through Lucy inspecting everything and giving her opinion on each purchase based on the packaging.

I lied to her yesterday, Róisín told him as they made their way to their desks.

You did not.

I did. I *have* seen the new colours in Penneys.

Manus' laugh went pealing out of him and he nodded gravely.

Don't give her an opening. Her mouth's like Gay Spar, it never closes.

They went their separate ways. She'd drifted into Comms: too much communication going on to use the full word. Sad, remembering her own line from years back. Whatsapp, she'd said, cos text messages contain too much information. They'd all laughed and a few weeks later she'd downloaded the app. Human rights orgs are built on the labour of interns. The intern killing fields, the desks across from her, had claimed a new victim. She watched the Intern. She looked Iranian, sounded Dublin 6. Don't exoticize her. She was gorgeous, doe-like, the office a novelty to her. Now she was looking at her too long. Princess Jasmin, run. Get out before it's too late. She should take her for a drink. She'd only put the fear of God in her. At eleven she met Manus by the imitation Nespresso machine.

Well, he said.

Didn't check the clock til quarter to ten.

Congrats.

Yeah, something to mention at my annual review.

She handed him a pod as she slotted hers in and it got punctured and the machine reared up. They took their time going back to their desks and Manus texted her at five to five.

– Pressing escape.

– On the way.

Together they stepped out into the busy street.

Listen they're doing this deal, Manus said. Pint and a moan for five fifty.

Maybe it's five fifty for the moan and the pint is consolation.

Maybe.

I can't, she said, I'm meeting a toddler for coffee.

They parted ways and merged with the city. She had nearly found the place when Lorna cancelled on her.

– Sorry babe. Just couldn't get the little one to sleep.

Little one fucked her off and being fucked off at natural cuteness aged Róisín and fucked her off even more. But we had talked through an avalanche of notions names for seven months. You finally landed on one now you don't even use it. He would have been Noah if he was a boy, Lorna had told Róisín, before it got too popular and they went off it. How many Noahs to a class. Southside saviour complex. Some halcyon green future where cycling would be enough. She regretted texting Lorna earlier in the week when she was full of good intentions, like the first week back to school. This was supposed to be working. The spectres of the girls from school were never far. Well done girls. Took your private education and your 500 points to Trinity and now you answer phones for google. She pictured herself in a draughty community hall, surrounded by beaten people in hard chairs staring at their shoes. It would be her turn to stand and they would welcome her and she would say my name is Róisín and I am a resentaholic. Lorna arranged to meet her on the weekend instead.

At home she boiled too much pasta and hid in her room. If she was given a quid every time she was told depression is like weather, she wouldn't be stressed over the rent. It passes, they said, but she knew that, she grew up with Irish weather so she knew that the rain was always coming back. She stared at Lorna's toddler on her phone. 'Getting started on the property ladder early' read the caption of Poppi by an IKEA playhouse. She scrolled on and saw Kathryn's newborn, then an image of Cliona frozen mid-leap on a beach stretching to the horizon, BRIDE stretched in gold caps across her chest. Don't read underneath the caption, she cautioned herself then she did it anyway: 'I can't believe it is a month since . . .' and she stopped before the hashtags. Maybe she'll post it every thirty days. Maybe this would never end. Your cloud storage is almost full. Her laptop was dying anyway. The screen glitched on her. She couldn't find anywhere right for herself in bed. She spent half the night awake mortified by previous transgressions. She hadn't been to the gym all week and her insides felt like pâté. She took a shower and hoped the day would circle the drain.

Look at daft.ie too much at night and wake panicked before there's colour in the day. She wrestled wet towels out of the washing machine. She made herself tea and looked at sheds and bunkbeds online that she could afford. She changed the search filters until finally they were kinder and she spent twenty minutes looking at places she would like to live and never would, then it was time to go to work. She flossed and bled. She didn't feel right.

Deadly buzz, Alex was saying to them. Alex was the MD. Manus said his type were a known issue and diagnosed him as symptomatic of gay men in their forties who spent outrageous money on rugs and swiftly pulled the ladder up.

Did I have a few Baby Guinness in PantiBar? Alex said. I just might have.

Behind Alex, Manus' eyes had nearly rolled completely into his head. Róisín snorted. The Intern beside her looked alarmed. The Intern was saddled with crushing amounts of admin. She was starting to struggle of late. Starting to realize this was all it was.

At lunch Róisín read the backs of packs in Marks and Spencer. That's the job she really wanted, rolling around delectable adjectives in your mouth, before she dragged herself back to the office. No Lucy on reception at least. Everyone else was already in. Róisín knew every muscle of her face was knotting, but knowing didn't help. Knowing and feeling were too far apart. She heard a distant war over the malfunctioning machines. Twitter accounts flagged the most outrageous shit up on daft.ie and she felt a curl of shame that she'd eagerly clicked on one of them this morning. Time was pressing in on her and she was doing nothing. Priced out of flat life and the office loved TOIL. She was trying to get some work done but Alex wasn't having any of it.

Have you put that in an email? he asked her.

I'm . . . I'm saying it to you, Róisín said.

Sorry. I'm not being clear. Could you put that in an email?

Does it need an email?

Course it does.

I just told you. So you . . . know about it?

Yes, I'm hearing you Róisín but I need you to put it into an email. Please. It's called procedure.

Ten feet apart, they sent passive-aggressive emails to each other for the rest of the afternoon. Alex could see her screen so she could only check for new places in stolen moments when he wasn't at his desk. Some people can live with their parents but nobody said anyone should or that anyone's parents were into it. There was no use talking to them, they thought liking anyone with politics any further left than their own parents had been enough. Crashes coming faster and faster. Her phone kept autocorrecting her own name to prison. She knew enough, that her parents waged minor, never-ending campaigns across restaurants and business parks. Now she could be the no-man's land in between, the scarred waste-ground. They could play football over her on Christmas Day, like smiling soldiers in a John Lewis ad.

Hope is a meeting. Hope is a meeting about a meeting.

It's evolution time, Alex was saying.

He moved to the flip chart. Róisín wondered if he had a matching flip chart at home where he wrote his weekend up.

We want to start moving towards something that's both universal and locally relevant. We're in the business of a solutions-focused hope slash change slash humanity message.

She felt Manus leaning in to her ear.

In fairness, he hissed, I fucking love it when it's solutions-focused.

OK hands-up time, Alex declared. Who wants to shape the future of our brand?

This kind of thing reminded her of sitting down the front at a stand-up gig. The horror. Hands shot into the air. Forever dreading being accused of a lack of enthusiasm, she slowly raised her hand.

She ate lunch on the boardwalk with Manus. A surly fat seagull eyeballed her.

I see you, she said. Bullies.

No such thing as a seagull, Manus said.

Ha?

They're all sea gulls. Like saying land human.

The wind lashed her hair about her face.

Oh, she said. I'm a bed human.

I've dreams, Manus said.

Do you now?

Yeah. Dreams of taking out the seagull coven at dawn.

Ha?

A gull cull.

Manus played up the shifty certitude of a man who's seen the light.

There must be one Queen Gull, he said. One enormous one.

She looked at him.

We should find her.

If we found her, would we have the heart to kill her?

Maybe not. Imagine how much grub she gets through in a day.

He stood and looked along the south quays towards the curving teals and further the rising steam from James's Gate.

Completely lost the run of themselves, he said.

o

I'm seeing a place later, she blurted and her mother sat up with new hope.

Oh good. Great, love. Can I see it?

No.

Sorry?

You don't want to see it, you just think you do.

By the time the bill was settled – Róisín just let her pay these days – her mother's eyes were fixed on the surrendered phone. Her mother brought the phone closer, peered into it, and her eyebrows climbed her forehead like shocked caterpillars.

No, her mother said softly to herself.

No what?

You can't live there.

I mean, I will if they let me.

A deep, exasperated sigh seeped from her mother.

It's a disgrace. When we were your age—

When you were my age you were making this mess.

Fine. Never mind.

'D'you remember when we were starving on Raglan Road?' Not sure it's any use to me.

Her mother asked her quietly to let her know how it went later.

Suitcases on wheels clacking and rolling down the street and she walked behind two gorgeous Italians in shiny bubble jackets, rides in unfortunate denim, him swinging a set of keys. She wondered if it was racist to hate tourists. The Luas took her through town. She was unnerved every time it stopped and she was sitting at eye level with everyone in the street. She got into a flurry of whatsapps with Lorna. She hadn't been asked to be the child's godmother two years ago though she was the obvious choice and it still chewed her.

The Jervis stop was as hectic and spicy as ever and she got off at Smithfield and walked into Stoneybatter. She turned another corner and left the redbricks behind. Renters loved redbricks. She was a renter. She needed to be renting. She could live here. She couldn't live here, she couldn't live anywhere, she'd be back with her parents and then she would watch them grow old in real time, like that seaweed that grows in front of your face. She tried to breathe. Be in charge of your own breathing, be in control of in and out. She tried to hold her tongue to the top of her mouth. There was a mass of people outside. She'd been at smaller demonstrations and she started to count them but that was impossible too, some couples, some with buggies, some knew each other and she knew that happened too, Lorna had told her stories of their nemesis couple, who turned up in all the houses they were viewing. There were eighteen now nineteen people outside. Two more made it twenty-one and everyone more suitable and groomed and she was shrunken and scared now, stopped and stooped and shaking. It was too much and she was too brittle, her nerves fracked, shrieking never ceasing and she couldn't go in now, couldn't walk around the house like the rest of them, imagining the home they would make it, moving around each other with plans and soft respect, her brain was teeth and cages and she had stopped dead in the middle of the street. A horn blared at her. She jumped as a car came for her. She stepped out of the way, and missed getting clipped by the wing mirror. The man in the car glared at her as he drove past. Everyone in the queue was staring and then it was full frenzy chest and shrunken shoulders. And now a baby was crying and fussed and hushed. She couldn't be anywhere. She wanted to lie down foetal on the pavement. She felt she was guiding herself away from this place, like a carer in a nursing home. She held on to herself, one thing at a time. It took everything she had, but she scurried away and into a coffee shop and when she got into a toilet stall she sat and shook. After a while her skin remembered it was on someone and that someone was her. On the bus she was quivering, nearly crying trying to get home. Her phone sprang messages from her mother.

– How'd it go? xx

She thought about telling her she'd found something at the end of the bus route. Ongar maybe. You can't leave your mother on read. You can though.

They took the Intern out on Friday, into the dark polished wood of the Swan. The relief of the week ending was all around them, but they took their pints outside and she faced towards the flats, her back to the drab workhouse of a church that hulked across the street. A taxi driver told her once Saint Valentine's bones were in there, preserved relics you could visit. The Intern scarred easy and told them she can't use any emoji she's used with any ex and a few weeks after their break-up, she was running out of emojis. Róisín thought she was joking.

My tits are ringing, the Intern yelped. She was right. She pulled a Samsung from between her breasts.

Just with work heads. No I'll come to you.

The Intern took herself off then, hopping up, phone wedged back into place.

Gang I'm ghost. See ya.

Off to Pyg with her, Róisín said as she watched her march back into town.

You keep getting older but they stay the same age, Manus said.

Pale and stale, she said.

Speak for yourself, hun, my flagrant faggotry absolves me. Listen.

He placed his palms on the table. Róisín realized he never looked guilty. Until now.

I'm leaving, Manus said.

What?

Yeah.

Fuck off, she said.

Yeah. Next month.

You can't leave.

No, that's just what they tell us.

He seemed so clear, a pure signal finding her through the din.

I can, he said. So can you.

Didn't know you were doing interviews.

He shrugged. He'd joined the dark side, a job in a new agency and it paid better. She pictured bean bags and slides. She wanted to be happier for him, but this came with gremlins. They were mandated to stay out now. This was the real leaving party.

Maybe it's giving up, he said. Don't know.

The most middle-class thing I ever did was believe in NGOs, she said.

When he went to the jacks, she looked at the website of the place he was going. Savvy sounders, it said, and showed pictures of open-plan offices, lush plants under ceiling ducts. The unmooring feeling was deeper than normal and there was nothing she wanted to check on her phone. You just had to get it a little bit wrong and it was too late. They found Manus' fella on Capel Street.

Drinking on my own here, he said, what you waiting for?

Waiting on the pay gap to close, Róisín said.

I'm waiting on the Apple millions myself, Manus said.
Manus kissed him. She went to get the drinks in but Manus
insisted.

We're all content pigs, honey, now get in the trough.
She got the next round in and they didn't eat and the three
of them floored juicy needy pints and she didn't remember
going home.

The next morning she opened one eye like a lizard and knew
she'd lost the day. Sent to the mines now. Only sent yourself to the mines. Awash with fear and blood she plugged
in her dead phone. She read messages she didn't remember writing and wished she could stay in bed. She dragged
herself up and into the shower and out. She was jumpy in
public as she climbed onto the bus. No driving licence. Now
scared of weekdays. Two Asian girls sat masked down the
back.
She got herself to Lorna's, her heart ratty and worthless, an
adolescent waiting outside her friend's new house. Lorna
looked fresh as she pulled the door back. She was still scratching at herself about why she wasn't asked to be godmother,
knowing in Lorna's eyes she was full proof right now. Inside
was like stepping into a magazine. The only people who buy
cookbooks are people who have too many cookbooks. Maybe
they had always valued different things.

We're going to play a game, Poppi told Róisín.
The two of them were sat in the front room. Lorna had gone
to make Poppi something to eat an aeon ago. Poppi was three,
a bright and toothy child staring expectantly at Róisín. The
game was snakes and ladders. She rolled again.

It's my game, Poppi said.

Róisín won the first time. Five minutes later Poppi changed the rules to ensure victory for herself.

And I'm the winner, the child said.

You're not the winner.

Suddenly Róisín saw her hand clamped over Poppi's little mouth, chipped nails and everything. She blinked, the thought gone, but Poppi seemed to sense what she was thinking, some animal instinct in her, and her fresh face took a bad turn and in seconds she was bawling. Lorna came running from the kitchen and Poppi explained, furiously pointing at Róisín with one paw, the other dragging long strands of snot and tears from her face. Her telling was shocked and urgent, words getting in the way of each other, full of mucus and betrayal. Lorna stared at Róisín.

Just let her win Ro, Jesus Christ.

Róisín stood up, trembling and staring at Poppi's snot. She turned and headed out of the room.

Where you going? Lorna demanded as she followed Róisín down the hall.

I need to get home.

But you haven't seen Poppi in ages.

Sure I see her loads online and I hit like every time too.

Why you being like this?

Because I'm not an entertainment system for your fucking toddler.

What?

She has an iPad she can use that.

What's my fault Ro? Tell me what's my fault.

She walked out and walked all the way home to the room she was running out of time in. Monday loomed, infecting the last hours of the weekend. She had not expected Sunday nights to feel like when she was in school.

o

In work people talked around her but she was unable to focus, unable to tell exactly who was speaking.

Let's talk about hope.

Yes!

She sensed time was stuck in a presentation about which was better, hope or humanity. Someone was lobbying hard for humanity, but for someone else it was all about the hope. She couldn't tune in to anyone.

Humanity isn't landing for me.

I hear you, something's not one hundred per cent.

I'm really feeling the hope buzz.

Like, it's hope, yeah?

Yes queen, Alex said.

Hope. Love it.

Hope lands.

Hope always works.

She spent Saturday packing, suitcases and bin bags heaped by the door. She trudged across the city. She hadn't told her parents she was coming and she sat bugged on the Luas out to Churchtown. The ray wing of the bridge ahead and she stepped onto the platform, hanging over the low dying shopping centre. The new mall, Dundrum Town Centre, had finished off the old one. She walked up the hill as cars passed her and then she stood outside the house. She held her finger just over the doorbell before she pressed it, turning to look at the street she grew up on. This is the view again. She heard her mother within. She turned around as her mother's eyes took her in then down to the bags around her daughter's feet.

I'm homeless, Róisín said.

No, you're not.

Her mother stepped back and ushered her in.

Won't be for long.

That's fine, love. Long as you need.

She climbed the stairs. They'd got rid of half her room, a weird hybrid now: her brother's pinned match tickets, her Less Stress More Success books. It was six years since she had lived in this room. At the window, the old familiar view out onto back gardens and trellises, a distant trampoline. She opened the window and leaned out. She heard a throat clearing and turned and her storky father appeared on the landing, in a navy shirt. It was still a novelty seeing him without a tie.

Oh, hello.

Hey Dad.

How'd you get all that back?

Got the Luas.

That's the green line.

Yeah.

Not the other one. The breadline.

He looked delighted with himself.

Oh my God, she said.

Nigel's line, I can't take any credit.

Watching your parents grow old in the same house as them. Turning old somewhere between them.

Being in the same room as someone else doesn't always mean a chat is necessary but her mother felt differently. Everything was spoken, everything read aloud, especially the whatsapps.

Mum, I'm in that group, she said.

Well we're not all glued to our phones all day.

Her mother spoke aloud each word she typed on her phone and Róisín closed her eyes.

o

Arthritis had her mother now and her hands turned in on themselves like the gnarled horns of a ram. Before any task, she ran them under hot water at the sink. Róisín watched her perform this new ritual of hers until she was finally able to run the zip up her jacket.

I'm going to the shops pet.

OK.

D'you want anything?

A fair rental market?

Her mother stopped zipping.

Smart's not always clever, d'you know that?

Everything was already rehearsed and most evenings framed a sincere and faithful restaging of old conflicts, all the lines learned, all each other's buttons worn and pressed.

Used to love getting home but you can't go home if you're always home. She hopped at every chance to get out of the office and had nearly forgotten she had a day at The Foundry and she enjoyed a different walk to work that morning. She shuffled into the looming auditorium. Hundreds of people faced the front as a confident young man bounded onto the stage. He clapped his hands with a sharp snap. He was beaming.

Morning Dublin. I've got one question for you. Who's ready for power breathing?

This was 'Breathing with Ronan'. Later they were told it's about the stories you tell. They broke for lunch. She realized with a shock of dread that Ronan himself was making a beeline for her. He had too much energy. She wondered if he was microdosing. Might just be the lifelong caffeinated confidence of private school coursing through him.

Saw you earlier, Ronan said. You coming in?

She shrugged.

Give you the tour?

Alright, go on so.

Let me just check it's kosher.

He moved to the door. A security guard lunked over. Some quiet words exchanged then some big laughs and shoulder pats for the gallery and it dawned on her that he wasn't allowed inside. He was trying to shrug off the awkward as he came back, laughing too much.

Shit, this is embarrassing, he said.

She kept her face blank and her tone light.

Not for me, she said.

He looked at her again, as if for the first time.

I'm really sorry about that.

You don't have to be sorry.

Ah I know. I don't have to be anything. What you doing this weekend?

Fuck all.

His beaming smile, a billboard before the invite.

D'you want to change that? he asked her.

Her laugh was a snouty thing and she didn't care.

Nope. Maybe one day they'll let you in.

She saw he was starting to take it in.

I better head, she said. See ya.

She got a roll in the sprawling Spar and ate it on the shelf looking out. The pleasing scald of coffee and she scrolled down the delights of her inbox. 'Please let me know if you want to be involved, but also please flag to me anyone else who you think has got the goods,' she read; 'I'm after campaigners, activists, supporters.' She read how they were very focused on getting an agency with a really global perspective, who will help them take the pulse right around the world.

o

It was officially a pandemic and someone had died on the island. Ski holidays and private school trips were bringing it back. She knew those trips and those schools. She'd gone to one of them. First snow that year, they'd be saying, girls like Alison McGuire and Sorcha Gorbally. She remembered them all, girls who seemed like their lives hit the slopes and never looked back.

RTÉ was an act of state aggression and never off.

It's men it's after, her mother said.

Bout time, Róisín said.

Her mother smiled.

Your father is self-isolating, her mother said.

Her mother was just shy of cocooning age but her dad was well into vulnerable territory.

He's very compromised, she said, and Róisín watched a bit of mischief playing around the corners of her mother's mouth.

Always was, she said.

On the news, seas of punters filled the Cheltenham grandstand. She watched her mother boil in her movements.

We're going to the shops, her mother said, fast and firm. It was Pac-Man in the SuperValu, reversing down the aisles to dodge people. Some covered their mouths, others sunk their heads down, their t-shirts hiked up over their noses. The shelves were plundered bare and hazmat white. Just when we couldn't do any more sorries, she thought, now this. They met each other in the wine aisle and loaded up. Next her mother was inspecting the avocados one by one. Probably Israeli avocados, Róisín thought, another thing not to mention. Her mother studiously pressed one, then another one.

She narrowed her eyes at the next avocado in her sights and leaned in, suspicious.

Ready to eat, they say, said her mother.

There was no need to be in here, trapped in the veg aisle, poking the avocados.

Well, I wouldn't eat that.

Extending a tightly wrinkled finger, her mother's single digit interrogated the surface of the avocado. This was not the time. The avocado was not the hill to die on. She fled and waited outside, frightened. Her mother appeared, laden with too many bags, just about able now but failing in future. Shamed and stung, Róisín went over and took half the bags from her protesting mother and they walked together to the car.

I'm doing a full minute, her mother said at home, nodding as she furiously scrubbed her hands.

You'll be drinking the Milton next.

No I won't be drinking the Milton next, thank you Róisín.

She brought her dad his dinner. She heard him from the other side of the door.

Dad, your fish heads are outside.

Thank you, love.

She left the plate and heard him from within.

My hat trick of recessions, he said as she turned for the landing. That's me done. Give me the match ball and let's call it a night.

Friday was the last day in the office. She sat beside Manus in the meeting. He scrawled a message for her on a branded notepad as Alex droned on: Covid 19 + Friday 13th = 32. She laughed. She got a sharp look from Alex. They decided not to go for pints.

That night she watched footage of emptied town. One prick bollock-naked in a deserted Temple Bar. She texted Manus. She usually texted him first.
– A stag during this. I nearly feel sorry for him.
– Fuck 'em. Temple Bar's been a containment pen for twenty years.
– Come out Tuesday, Paddy's Eve.
– Maybe.

The Tories put up a press release behind a paywall, Broken Brexit brain devouring its young.

On Sunday she sat beside her mother for the state of the nation, the Taoiseach slick and smug, his voice a dripping thing. Her dad had gone to the same school.
　　You don't have to say anything Róisín, her mother said. Just watch the news.
She stayed on her phone with Manus throughout.
– Thinks he's Churchill.
– Not all heroes wear capes.
– Can't go out tonight now anyway. I cringed so hard my skin fell off.

The best pubs were the first to close.

It was here now, it was everywhere. Think as if you have it. Don't touch your face.

Working from home. Living at work.

o

She missed hearing people in other rooms, like they were just there, just inside, and you could go back into them and they'd want to hug you. She cruised twitter bios of men she hated, the bile rising at all the future CEOs. Someday you'll buy a pizza from me, she read. Boys make such weird threats.

She heard her mother's voice in her head even when she wasn't speaking. Sometimes she wondered whether it was in her own skull. Can't hear yourself think. Most of it fades off, just the nails remain.

Military helicopters landing in the Phoenix Park.

Glove Life, snapping them on to go to the shops.

The fake news whatsapps, and explaining them to her mother.

Field hospitals in car parks and along the quays. Coffins for Italians.

Making a mental list of who's zoomable, instead of who's fuckable, is a lot less craic. Every bus was empty. She watched the news with her mother and when the monster came on her mother muted him.

May god forgive me but I hope he gets it.
They ordered masks. She hadn't gone out in days. Much of it suited her.

Life got blocked into little screens, watery sound, stuck in delay and glitching again. She mostly watched other people watching other people. Wrecked after, she helped herself back into bed. It had always been March.

Couldn't remember if you had that argument this morning or four weeks ago, so you had it again.

Her sixth zoom of the day. She blinked. Her eyeballs were dry.

I know there's a lot of takeaways for us in these strange times. I want to really thousand-per-cent these days, you know? You get me Róisín?

I think so.

Manus told her in town it was tricolours out the windows. Not in Churchtown. Her dad had a video from his friend Nigel. She watched at his elbow: huge houses with older men stood proudly outside, singing the plastic anthem from the rugby internationals.

Oh my god. It's not even the anthem, she said.

Her dad mouthed along.

More deaths and she went on twitter like a video game you couldn't win. The arse had fallen out of Airbnb and landlords were promising mints on pillows and mini toiletries for short-term rents.

Miriam was on the Late Late, because Tubridy was on holiday. Róisín remembered him talking about Greta, saying she was a child who needs to be brought home and this too she kept to herself.

First woman ever, hosting it, her mother said, On the longest running show ever, they said.

Their phones on the couch buzzed in sync. The text came from within the house.

You look at it, her mother said.

Not the longest running show ever, he says.

Their phones buzzed again.

He has a link in it.

Let him.

The slowest exhale from her mother.

We should stop feeding him, her mother said.

On the news grandparents stood dumb on the wrong side of a fence from their grandkids, looking at their children like cows in a field. Less reason for her mother than ever to think she'd be a grandparent. Zombie cans in bed, talking to Manus after.

Any news, he asked.

My mother is a Zoom Queen. My Father is a Meme Lord. And you?

Suppose I've been taking the end of the world seriously.

Drama much?

She hung up first but they arranged to meet.

Domestic violence up, like after matches. We are right to be scared.

On the landing she found her dad in a salmon jumper squinting to examine the ceiling light.

You know, I'm always surprised we're still in this house, he said.

What?

This was only supposed to be our starter home.

Read the fucking room, Dad.

I had plans, he said.
She slammed her door.
We can all slam doors, love.

See the numbers, they asked each other every evening. Death bingo.

Lucy the receptionist rang, just checking in with everyone. Róisín did not mention her afternoon collapse.

House of Lady Macbeths, everyone up all hours, competitive hand washing.

She left various people on read: Manus, her book club, her brother.

Every day the same except the numbers went up. Hand sanitizer robbed from a funeral.

Bed is self-care. Time was broken now. Suspected she was too caustic for real life anyway.

The pangolins had done her a solid, if they were the carriers. Pokémon-looking motherfuckers who never asked to be eaten in wet markets. Sarkymon, I choose you.

The sun came out Friday. She milled wine with her parents and ate Bombay Pantry. She got a text when she was already stuffed with naan, only her father still eating. It was Lorna.
– Fancy a zoom? Me and the girls are hopping on.
– Sure.

She hauled herself up to the room, glass in hand, the food coma incoming.

Don't leave me in the waiting room ladies.

Going to be a lot of pandemic babies.

I got furloughed, Lorna said.

You mean fired, Róisín said.

Sorry, I'm furloughed Róisín? Thanks.

What's the difference?

Róisín knew what she had said as it all froze and she waited to have to deal with it again. She thought about hitting red and running. She waited for their faces to come back and turn sour.

Sorry, Róisín said.

It's been tough for you, I know. With your mental health.

Róisín get away from the window, her mother said.

In case it sees me?

There's people dying out there.

Róisín looked out but saw no corpses. A Volvo rolled by.

These were our holiday years, her mother said.

Together they watched emptied-out moonlit piazzas, abandoned Italian cities on webcam.

Your father loves Rome.

Her mother stood up then sat down again. She studiously typed out a message, a frown of concentration on her face.

We'll never get away again, her mother said to herself.

Ah come on.

I'll be too old and he'll be too dead.

The stale drift. The Last Dance or Normal People.

o

She moved around the bones on her plate. Finished the porn she liked and some she didn't. Single wouldn't be fixed this month. The ex would do at this stage. Could sneak him down the side passage when the parents went for their constitutional. Get him inside and get him inside her then get him out. Toss him after. The last time they met crept around her head. You can't share that pain.

Now we must face it alone.

Maybe never get the ride again.

This summer of rubble.

We the virus.

The thin paper her mother held in her hands like a loss. There is no news anymore, there is only one news. Slowly cracking in bright spring. She kept looking out but no towering evil came looming over the rooftops. Occasional chirp of bird. Her dad bounded down the stairs and into the kitchen.

You're looking lively, her mother said.

That's enough of that room, he said. Who wants to go for a walk?

Me, me.

She watched her mother, a woman who had put fifty thousand miles on the clock driving them round but had never walked for pleasure, hurry to get her coat. They took off quickly and left her alone in the house. She had to stop finding plague before anything funny. Plague year. Plague crisps. She hit the heart on Lorna's picture of Poppi and left a comment. Baby's first plague.

Manus told her to meet him at the park. She felt covert and guilty walking over to him. He brought cans but no news from town. He said in the charity shop windows it was still Paddy's Day.

Only addicts digging in bins and Deliveroos bringing people takeaways, that's it.

Where you going to go?

Not home. Wouldn't even be the only gay if I went back. There'll be some fresh-faced brat on the come up.

We're ancient.

Yeah, but y'know what? I'm not sorry.

No.

Not sorry for every stupid night, he said.

I just feel sorry for anyone who did dry January.

Yeah, where's your smug now, bitch.

You might like being home.

No! he roared. No. This tired fossil queen, back from the city, he said. No. I hope it takes me first. Dublin's as small as I can live with.

Two Guards advanced on them then, blocking out the sun and looking up, they shaded their eyes.

Only out exercising Guard.

Exercising is it?

Yes Guard, Manus said. Exercising my right to drink cans in the park.

Empty your bag there.

She couldn't help giggling. The Guard frowned and stepped closer. Now he was just a great dark shadow above her, all sunlight gone and her head was fizzy.

Sorry, Róisín said. This makes me feel young.

The Guards made them pour out their cans and they were cleared out of the park.

Don't ever apologize to them, Manus said.

You're right.

Anything I want to do is self-care. Everything I'm not let to is deplatforming.

Guards being pricks . . .

I mean nature's healing.

Yeah. If nature heals anymore my hymen will grow back.

He screamed and threw his head back in buzzy delight. She left him at the park gate and wandered home.

No more zoom invites from Lorna. Like searching for something you knew you'd written down somewhere. That night she left the house and walked through the suburban silence. Some kids were drinking in the graveyard. She stood in the middle of the road before the bridge. Each car could be heard coming from miles away. Traffic lights changed for nothing and no one. If you run, you can run in the middle of the road now and never need to look over your shoulder.

She walked back to the house. Sat in the kitchen with her mother and twirled the long grey hair that had recently started leaving her face. A day ago maybe. Maybe a week. They had tea. Something to do.

I could grow it, Róisín mused.

What's that love?

My beard. Like a way of marking time . . .

She tilted her head back, detached and precise, hoping to elongate it.

You're getting worse, her mother said.

Watched by her mother, Róisín lifted up the open laptop to carry it with her out of the room.

It's a wonder you don't take it into the bath with you, she said.

It's that or the toaster.

Her mother's face jacked up in sharp shocks and she started crying. Róisín looked out to the garden, manicured and beginning to bloom, still aware of the small shrewy sounds emanating from the crumpled shape of her mother. She put the laptop down and went over. Her mother stopped her with a small hand.

I'm sorry, Róisín said.

But it's always. You're always at it.

We are.

Her mother sat up straight, wiped her face and with her sorry, wounded look stung Róisín.

No, love. It's you. It's really you.

Another morning and she slowly tuned into her mother's voice after coffee sharpened her. A distant cousin had died.

RIP.ie doesn't even have the church or a date on it.

Drowning in quicksand. It was Wednesday. Or November. The Smudge.

Later she heard her mother on zoom with her sisters, laughing like girls.

She was eating smoked salmon. Slimy slick pleasures. It was pretty comfy for an apocalypse. In the kitchen her parents were giddy, trailing hands and touching each other. She was at the table between the two of them and they were drinking too much but she could say nothing. She was taking the bait at everything her dad said. She exhaled enough that even her dad realized it was meant for him.

What's wrong now?

She said nothing.

It's easy to be a creep now, her dad said.

She felt her skin shrivel. She would outlive them. She could feel her dad rise to open another bottle. Her mother was in a silk dressing gown she'd never seen before.

Used to be, it was almost impossible.

That's what made you all creeps.

Maybe so.

Did you see this one? she asked and moved closer to him. No?

Then she ripped the phone from his hand and flung it hard straight down onto the kitchen tiles. It smashed, bits flying to different corners. Silence now coating the bits on the floor. You did all this, politely. You stopped nothing. Now it's too late. The dad curse is believing you did something, our curse is knowing it meant nothing. In the end nothing. Her mother will want for nothing. She wanted for nothing herself.

Death roads ahead. Truth was she kinda loved it. Weird buzz watching awful shit on the news. Little bit gorgeous. Let the world be hard on itself. She checked her phone. Was it for likes. We get our memes and the burning earth, and we'll take it til the internet goes off and it'll be too late.

She had an extra bottle stashed in the room: bleak rebellion, drinking wine in your childhood bed at twenty-nine, watching documentaries on youtube. She could see the countdown to the interrupting ads coming, in 3, 2, 1 . . .

Suddenly a muscled American was shouting at her. He was selling a jaw product. He had something like a dog toy in his mouth.

I literally rolled back the hands of time, the man said. He said the chew yoke held forty pounds of resistance. She looked at before and after shots of his tanned jawline at the same time. She slammed the laptop and stood. She closed her door, turned the light off and in search of company, followed the sound of muffled music. As she padded downstairs, she could hear one of her dad's albums playing, crooner lines about starting over. Halted when she saw the two of them on the couch, clothes half off – her dad was angrily spidered on top of her – and he had his mouth on her nipple and his tongue going round on it. Her dad was finger banging her mother, his veiny piston of an arm firing in and out of her and the wet sucking sound and her low moans. Róisín's breath pushed the room away. Her mouth curled into an ugly thing. Her mother opened her eyes to see her but her dad did not stop and now her fists clenched and her veins boiled. Now her sweating parents flung themselves to other sides of the couch. On her way out she reefed the volume up on the snared teens. The house would be in division. This would be her house in time. She stepped outside and walked into the dusky greens of the back garden, the sky murking overhead, and sat on a deckchair.

They were getting younger. Maybe they'd start an onlyfans.

She might stay out for the evening. The weather was warming up, the nights getting longer.

She had all the time in the world to go back in.

People disappear.

They just drop through the cracks.

Everyone talking your language and the world catching up.

ghost trails

When you move in your sleep I worry
know something you're dreaming is scaring you,
think you know with every turn
think it's me,
Think it's something I've done
You're right.
The time together lives on in our skulls, dragged over old
    laughs, smiles wrapped around you, left your heart
    a quarry.
When you've turned over, when you're on a different
    page now.
When it switches between us and
when it's switched off.
You can't tell someone how much hurt lives, that only
    births more hurt into the world,
so you live it down inside yourself and it sinks and stings
    and stinks of you.
Came up out of you sometimes, little hops from your
    throat.
Back when you first came in and stole the room,
You held glances that told you it could work that you could
    wake together and have your future flower,
Good luck with that.

Are we better now

Colder but cleaner

Less angry now it's lost.

Still signed in as us

Could see what movies you were watching but mostly
    abstained,

Never stressed about catching feelings

always got in straight away

Always took their hands and carefully closed them over
    your trachea

Helped them choke you with their caring.

Too late for anyone else you started painting them with all
    the colours of your affection

Stuck on haunted by the ghost, laughing

Fuck else would haunt you, you said

Only one of us here

Never kept anything said, just the damp in the moment

Course arguments flared and dimmed, mad fires in your
    flat but the months washed them all away left you with
    something smaller and softer, seeping tidal sores,

a little cyst of affection.

Bad at pulling away and scared of slow
Holding someone's face is a terrible act,
The raw ask of your eyes and too many times you looked
    away
Made a deal out of nothing and hurt you.
Never meant to.
Had you racing, bailing towards conclusions and walks in
    Connemara, pints shine and chowder,
Home after fat weekends to a gaff on a street a hundred
    years old and the world would roll past outside in the
    evenings, away from us.
Changes nothing, you said. You still did it. Won't help now.
Still brought your name up more than you should.
Ashamed at the rush of your name scrolling
Traps everywhere, your days office-claimed
You got sucked in, got gleeful in it one night in winter
    opening yourself to the small chance there's other ways
    of being happy
There's other arms at night and other smiles in the
    morning
Under the cathedral and that nearly happened somewhere
    else,
So many streets, you said, remember.
Felt like school when you woke up.

You know it won't happen.
You won't say it back, won't give it back.
Left us both hanging off the silence.

When it's a broken after,
Where there's space for doubt now and it starts to rot
    and hatch and eat
Left with yourself
If that's when you trusted yourself, who else could
Still shaking, searing dead-end fights
Always snagging in your head catching, bitching at yourself
    before you said a thing
Never wronged still made you feel like it
Sit in unsaid shit, shouting violent silence
That couple for other couples to know and knowing it
    helped nothing now
Every thought trapped in the maze of us,
So you said nothing.
Don't remember much of the end,
Only remember you looked so small, a sudden hurting
    animal.
How many times can you each say I don't know until you
    both realize you do
You do know
You both know.

Be easier if one of us was dead.
A part of you grew into me
Less of me now and maybe you were better off before,
When you knew less, when we'd never met.
Ran out of time. Or your time anyway. Ran us out of
    your time.
Back when we each had a shot at fixing each other.
Start looking at the cracks and fissures in yourself.
Hoped you were only found out in parts and never wholly
    uncovered
Maybe they saw it all straight off and held it from you even
    as you fell fast
Run scenes on loop, only shaking pain wrenched up.
But had to be you sometimes
Wasn't wrong every Saturday.
Last nights and last words,
Expiry dates creeping round the back of things
Wouldn't come home that night
Or couldn't you said,
Fuck off and sort yourself, you never said
Must have thought it.
Months off but maybe only months
The weeks grew
Here's your space and here's your time
Now fill it up, prick.

Buried that place on your chest
Snuffed out the only body in the world you chose never to
    sleep next to again.
No crying if you're holding the machete.
Snagged by it anywhere
lamplit corner, snatch of song, a restaurant we never got to
Never reckoned a jar in the back of the fridge could find you
    in heart trouble
Emboldened by the light of dreams you torched your
    good thing
Paid for it now.
Bear it in hiding.
Someone to vanish the rest.
Trust your gut your friends said but where does that
    leave you
Your gut's cruel, your gut's a nasty bollix
Everyone walks,
Everyone walks until someone doesn't.
Can't see you ahead the way you see me.
Try walk it off, wear it down and wear it out of you
From the island at night the sea is huge and dark
Almost all gone now.
Savage nights vanished.
Less every time.
Praying for your voice to fade.

Months later still skinned.
Walk around in it, your breathing changing
Would you want a reason?
Still got the dog heart, still landed scars red and welting
You had to ask, know that now, place no blame in it.
The only person you can talk to about it, the only one
    who'd know, stay quiet.
Natural light never got a look in, never gave it a chance to,
Just the tearing slow grind, learning to live without the play
    of your sour breath.
Maybe they did you a favour calling it early
Maybe it wasn't early
Maybe they're wrong.
But someone you love is wrong
About you
makes no odds anyway.
You're not good enough
You're not right enough
In the end they don't want you
You've to respect that and respect yourself in that
Fall to other plans now,
Never made any.

Said your name softly still,
Charming lines that never found you
Still making air with the idea of you
Knowing what you'd say to things you never said
Can't stop it, currents unknowable.
No stopping land of look behind
Later the laptop suggested you, your guttered heart fuel
    for algorithms
It's all after
You out there, fifteen-minute walk away, five minutes' run,
    thinking the same
And you could text but you won't
Could call but you won't
So we stay in our sores and our rooms and we wait.
Cockroaches and crisis actors.
adidas Originals are still made in sweatshops, lovers.
Tropical storms after everything collapsed into itself.
In the pissings of June rain,
Time gone and about time,
Shrinking from the downpour, stuck hot
Where it was us before
Could have been anywhere.
After the us.

When it blazed between us at the top, gliding around with it
Matching each other
Holy nothing time
When we mattered.
What have you forgotten compared to us
But we happened, it was no one else
When it sparked, right when we hadn't had a chance to be
    wrong yet
Later no amends would be enough and we'd learn to live
    with less grace
Names of dead lads in your phone.
I love you or I'm scared
I love you and I'm scared
Just lost each other
Forever lost to each other.
Guess you didn't trust your luck
Older, other lives hushed down inside ourselves
They danced in their cages and you walked the halls again.